NOWHERE CHILD

Nowhere Child

A Short Novel

Rachel Abbott

NOWHERE CHILD

Find out more about the author and her other books at
http://www.rachel-abbott.com

ISBN-13: 9780957652255

Author's note

Dear Reader,

Thank you for choosing to read *Nowhere Child*!

Some of you will be interested in this story because you have already read *Stranger Child* and you may be one of the many people who contacted me to ask what happened next to Tasha Joseph.

Others may be coming to Tasha's story for the first time, and if so I hope I have written this novella in a way that will satisfy you. But if this book leaves you keen to find out what happened to Tasha before the start of *Nowhere Child* and what led to her running away, the answers lie in *Stranger Child*.

With best wishes,

Rachel Abbott

1

It's quiet tonight in the tunnel. It's because we're so cold. We sit huddled in our little groups around fires that we know won't last long. Andy has lit ours in an old, rusty, catering-size tomato tin that he found outside a restaurant. With a couple of holes punched near the bottom it gives off a bit of heat, although it will soon burn the small amount of fuel we have. We can always get paper to burn, and the brief, bright yellow flame is comforting, but it only lasts a few seconds. Wood is harder to find. The freezing November wind is bouncing off the damp walls, hitting us in icy blasts as if someone keeps opening and closing a door. But there isn't any door – just a gaping black hole.

There are four or five groups of us down here, sitting in twos and threes huddled around our feeble fires. We keep to ourselves mostly. I can see the odd face, lit from below by the weak yellow flames, features hovering, disembodied, against the black walls, the eyes hollow pits. I can hear the occasional murmur of conversation but mostly I listen to the steady drip from the roof. It is relentless, and I'm not surprised when Andy says that dripping water is used as a form of torture. Another drop joins in, this time with a slightly different tone. There is a pause, and for a second I wonder if it's stopped. But of course it hasn't. *Drip-drop. Drip-drop.*

I pull the last bit of chicken from the bone with my teeth. It's another great find of Andy's. He hangs around outside the back of a posh restaurant most days and just dives in when food is thrown into the bins. People leave so much on their plates.

I shuffle a bit closer to the fire, and Andy smiles at me. We look out for each other, but he's a bit older than me, so I always feel I've got the better deal. However bad things get, he's always laughing and he mucks about, exaggerating his Scottish accent to make me giggle. Whenever he is puzzled by something, he rubs his hand backwards and forwards over his straight ginger hair, making it stick up on top. It's grown long and covers his ears now. He seems older than his years, but when he doesn't know I'm watching, he sometimes looks a bit sad and lost.

I don't know what his story is but I do know that at some time in his life he has broken his arm because it's set at a funny angle. Whatever happened, he can't have gone to hospital, or it wouldn't be like that. We don't ask each other questions, but he knows I'm not who I pretend to be, just as I know that something terrible has happened to him.

I haven't been to the surface for days, but there are some people down here and in other parts of underground Manchester who haven't been above ground for years. Andy says at one time there was a whole community – about eighteen thousand people – living underground in Manchester back in the nineteenth century. I don't know if I believe him.

I can hear a louder voice at the end of the tunnel. It must be somebody new, because there's something about this place that makes us all talk in low voices – or not talk at all. The newcomer is getting closer to us. He's stopping at each pitch, crouching down and asking questions. I look at Andy and somehow I know. So does he. I can't run, though – the guy would catch me in a flash.

Slowly, silently, I shuffle back from the fire into the shadows. The orange flames are still lighting Andy's face, but mine is hidden. My hoody is a bit big, so I pull the hood as far over my head as I can. I always wear boys' clothes now, and my hair is less than an inch long all over. When I can, I dye it – but it grows out quickly, and there are only so many places that I can nick the dye from. It's not good to keep going back to the same shop.

I can see the newcomer in the distance, and as far as I can tell from here he looks like a young bloke, maybe mid-twenties. He's tall, but he seems top heavy because he's wearing a dark-coloured puffa jacket and he's got skinny legs that look a bit bandy to me. I thought when they came for me it might be somebody I would know, but it isn't, and that's good. Less chance he will recognise me.

He's showing something to the people next along from us, and I feel myself start to sweat even in this icy cold.

Now he's moving towards us. If I keep my head down completely it will seem very suspicious, so with my hood as far over as is sensible I rest my chin on my knees, wrap my arms around my shins and pretend to be staring into the fire. Unless he lies down, he won't be able to see my eyes.

I desperately want to look at him, so I'll know him if I see him in the street, but I can't look up. All I see are his feet – newish trainers, navy-blue with white soles – and his jeans – tight and dark. Definitely not a homeless guy, then. And I was right about the legs.

'Hey,' he says to Andy. He fishes a piece of paper out of his pocket, and I know what it is. There are thousands of them flying around Manchester. It's a poster with a photo of me on it.

Andy grunts a response and carries on pretending to poke the fire with a piece of iron he found somewhere.

'Do you know this girl, kid?' he says to Andy. Andy pretends to look at the poster and pulls a face.

'Nah – she's not round here or I'd have seen her.'

'What about your pal here?' He starts to move towards me.

Casually, Andy holds out a hand and takes the paper, distracting the man.

'What's all the fuss about this wee lassie anyway?' he says. 'I've seen lots of these bits of paper in the wind. What's the story?'

The man's attention is diverted from me for a moment.

'She's just another runaway, but there are people that want her found – and they're offering a reward.'

I freeze. This is a new development. If there's a reward, people are going to be far more interested. It's only natural.

'Yeah? How much?' I hear Andy ask. *Oh no, not you, Andy.*

'Five grand,' the man says, 'and if you help me find her, you can have a cut too.'

'Fifty fifty?' Andy asks.

The man laughs. 'We'll see – just find her first.' He looks towards me again.

'It's no use asking Harry,' Andy says. 'He's not been above ground for months and he don't speak much. I just look out for him. He's only a bairn – just eleven last week.'

The man loses interest in me, and I feel a stab of guilt that I ever doubted Andy. I'm not eleven, of course, but I'm very thin so I could easily pass for younger than I am.

'Well, just keep your eyes open and let me know if you see her – I'll give you my number.'

'Ah, right. I'll just be using my brand new iPhone to call you, will I?' Andy's humour is not lost on the man.

He laughs. 'There's phone boxes, thicko, and you can always nick enough to make a call, I'm sure. Here, I'll write it on the flyer for you.'

He scribbles the number on one of the sheets of paper he pulls from his pocket.

'I'll be back in a day or two – see if anybody's seen her.'

With that, the man moves off further in the tunnel.

We wait in silence until he is well out of earshot.

'Do you want to tell me what's going on?' Andy asks. 'You don't have to if you don't want, but there's always people looking for you. The woman who hands these out, for one.' He waves the piece of paper at me. 'She's been looking for you for months. The cops were asking around, too, though that was a while back. And now this guy today.'

'I ran away.' Andy wants an answer, but it's all I can give him. 'I'm just a missing kid like you are.'

Andy laughs. 'You don't see nobody offering a reward for me, do you?'

I just smile at him. I want to tell him, but how can I? How can I say that the woman looking for me is my stepmother, Emma, and she's looking for me because I stole her baby? My own brother.

2

The visitor last night scared me. I don't know what to think. I need to know if Emma has got some daft notion in her head that she can offer a reward for me. Surely she would realise that it could be dangerous – that the wrong people would be interested? But she doesn't know what the streets are like and what people might do for money.

I don't understand why she would do it now, though, after all this time. It doesn't make any sense. But I need to know, so when I woke up this morning I decided I had to leave the tunnel and try to find out what's happening.

I've seen Emma before, watched her from the distance, but she's never clocked me. I don't think she would recognise me now. No more straggly blonde hair. I look like a boy, and that's the plan – I don't want anybody to know who I am.

I don't know how often she comes into Manchester but I know she doesn't always go to the same part of town. Sometimes she's up in Piccadilly, other times she's in King Street or Market Street. She carries a yellow plastic box with her, upends it on the floor and stands on it to make her taller than the passers-by. And she always has Ollie with her; lovely Ollie, with his round, smiling face and his pudgy cheeks; the very same Ollie that I stole from her.

The thought makes me shudder.

I start looking for her in Piccadilly Gardens. She's not here yet, but I know she often stands on some steps that lead up to a statue, so I move over to the far side so she won't be able to see me.

I can smell pizza, and it's nearly killing me. My belly doesn't rumble any more – it's way past that stage – but the longing for a huge meal that would make me need to lie down and nurse my bloated belly is sometimes overpowering. A boy walks past, eating a burger, cheese and grease oozing from the bread bun, and I want to steal it out of his hands and run. But I can't draw attention to myself.

After an hour I give up and start to make my way down Market Street, past the trams and into the pedestrian bit. That's when I hear her.

'Tasha! Tasha Joseph,' she's shouting. 'We miss you. Ollie misses you too.'

Then I hear Ollie's squeaky little voice. 'Tasha!' He can make the 'sh' sound now. He used to call me Tassa. My eyes fill with tears, but I brush them quickly away.

Emma looks great. She's got a bright-blue coat on over jeans tucked into flat boots and a stripy scarf round her neck. Her dark hair is shorter, just resting on her collar, and it suits her. I can't see Ollie because he's in his pushchair – I can just see the tops of the handles. I want to get closer, but I daren't.

I listen to her shouting about how she's trying to find me, and how she wants me to come home, and it's so very tempting. But she can't mean it – not after what I did. People are looking at the hand-outs and then just dropping them on the floor. Nobody gives me a second look.

I edge a little closer and duck into the entrance to a sports shop, trying to get a glimpse of Ollie. I can see him now. There's a black and white spotted blanket over his legs and tucked up under his arms. He's wearing a blue knitted hat that's pulled down over his ears, and his little cheeks are a bit pink with the cold. But he's getting a lot of attention, and loving it.

Suddenly his head swivels in my direction, as if he can feel my eyes on him. He can't recognise me, though. I've got Andy's black baseball cap on with the visor pulled down. I'm dressed like a boy and I look so different. He can't possibly know it's me.

Emma looks down at her son, and she follows his gaze. I'm sure she can't see me, but she starts to climb down from her box, her eyes fixed on mine, a puzzled expression on her face. I look away and stare into the shop through the open door, as if I'm waiting for somebody. I glance sideways at the window in the entrance, and it forms a mirror of the street behind me. I can see that Emma has grabbed Ollie's pushchair and she's coming towards me.

I've got two choices. I can either go into the shop or leg it up the street. If I go into the shop, the security guys will be watching me. It's the way I look – they will be expecting me to nick something. If I move out into the light, Emma will see me properly, and she'll know.

I hesitate for a moment too long, then push myself off the glass wall of the entrance and out into the street. I turn my head away so she can't see my face and run as fast as I can.

She starts to shout, telling people to stop me, but nobody does. One guy half-heartedly puts an arm out, but I push it out of the way and I can almost feel him shrug as if to say, 'I tried.' But he didn't really.

I know Emma can't chase me. She can't leave Ollie. I don't know if she can be sure it was me – but she saw my eyes. And, however strange I look, she will know there was something – some spark of recognition.

I shouldn't have come. It would have been better for everybody if Emma thought I'd gone away. Or better still, that I was dead.

3

'Tom – are you there? It's Emma. I need to speak to you. It's urgent.' There was a pause, as if she was waiting for the phone to be picked up. 'I've seen her, Tom. I've seen Tasha.' Emma spoke quickly, breathlessly, as if the excitement was too much.

There was a frustrated tutting sound. 'Come *on*, Tom. Pick *up*.'

Detective Chief Inspector Tom Douglas stood at the open door to the back garden, where he had been enjoying a quiet beer in the cold fresh air of a November evening, an infrared heater keeping the worst of the chill at bay.

He didn't move towards the phone. He needed to think about what he should say to Emma – what advice to offer her. She had always had a determined streak in her – an aspect of her personality that Tom had admired all those years ago when she had been engaged to his brother Jack. At times Tom had believed Emma was the only thing that had kept his brother's feet on the ground. She and Tom had grown close then, and since they had been back in touch in recent months they had become good friends again.

He knew she would be thrilled to have seen Tasha after all her efforts to find the girl, but she seemed to believe it was all going to be so simple, and Tom knew she was wrong.

In the eight months since her stepdaughter, Natasha, had gone missing, Emma had been relentless in her search for the girl. For the first few weeks, or maybe even months, Emma had travelled into Manchester or Stockport at least three times a week, handing out posters with pictures of Natasha – or Tasha as she was more generally known – begging people to help her find the girl.

Tom had tried to warn her that even if she found Tasha, it might not be possible for her to adopt the girl. Emma may have been married to David – Tasha's father – for a few years but Tom didn't think that would count. Had he still been alive it would have been a different matter, but David was dead, and Tasha probably didn't even know it. Given their history, who knew what the courts would say?

His thoughts were interrupted by a disappointed sigh.

'Okay – you're obviously out. I'll call you back – but please, if you get this message will you call me? I really need to speak to you.'

The line went dead, and Tom felt a stab of guilt. Emma needed him. But he had to work out what to say to her before calling her back. He didn't want to quash her enthusiasm or put a dampener on things, but he had been begging her to think this through for months. Her answer was always the same.

'I know she ran away – but we have to look at it from her point of view. We'd only had her back for a few days – and what a terrible few days they were. I'm sure she thought she had no other choice but to run. She'll have assumed I'd never forgive her for taking Ollie. I've got to find a way to let her know that she's wrong.'

Tom went to grab his beer from the garden, turned off the heater and came back inside. He pulled out a stool and sat at the central unit, resting his elbows on the work-surface. He took a swig from the bottle.

It was all so complicated. Since being abducted at the age of six, Tasha had endured a terrible few years in the care of a member of an organised crime gang, being forced to shoplift and ferry drugs. Now there was nobody left to assume parental responsibility for this child – to make decisions for her – and so it would come down to the local authority and what they believed to be in the child's best interests. She still had family on her mother's side, but when Emma had approached them to ask for help in finding Tasha, they had made it clear that she wasn't part of their family any more. Her grandfather had made the decision and instructed his family to abide by his wishes.

'We lost our granddaughter the day her mother died. The child is a criminal now,' he had said. 'Nothing is going to change the way she has been brought up during those formative years, and it's best she sticks to the life she knows.'

That was it – all he'd had to say on the matter. Emma hadn't spoken to Tasha's family since.

Tom picked up the phone and dialled a number. It was answered almost immediately.

'Becky, how up to speed are you in the details of the search for Natasha Joseph?' he asked without further introduction. Becky Robinson was a detective inspector on his team and had been closest to the Joseph family during the events eight months previously.

'Hi Tom. Just give me a sec while I turn the TV down.' There was a brief pause as the background noise came to an abrupt end. 'Okay – Tasha Joseph. I've been keeping an eye on progress – I had a look earlier today, actually. But we don't seem to be making much headway, I'm afraid. Not a peep from anybody. Why the special interest now?'

'I've just had a call from Emma. She thinks she's seen Tasha.' He heard an intake of breath from Becky.

'That's brilliant news, Tom, if it's true. Do you think it really was her, or is it wishful thinking on Emma's part?'

'She seemed fairly convinced.'

'Where was Emma when she saw her? It will help us hugely in focusing the search, and we're running out of time. We're lucky that we've had this long to try to find her.'

'I don't know where she was, because I'm ashamed to say I didn't answer Emma's call – I just listened to her message. I'm finding it hard to deal with her optimism about Tasha.'

Tom took a final mouthful of his beer.

'That poor kid.' Tom could hear the genuine sympathy in Becky's voice. 'I wonder what she's thinking?'

'God knows. I should imagine she's lost, lonely, scared and probably confused about why Emma is looking for her. I'll have a think about the best way to show Emma some restrained enthusiasm, and then I'll call her back and find out where she saw Tasha. I'll let you know, and let's hope we find her.' He ended the call and threw his beer bottle in the recycling bin.

He couldn't ignore the fact that they needed Tasha. She was a vital witness in a trial that was due to start just one week from today.

4

Andy has gone to try to find us something to eat. Neither of us has eaten a thing all day, but I don't feel hungry – just empty. There's a massive hole where my belly should be and it feels as if all the water I've drunk is just sloshing round in there on its own. I picture it like a washing machine, splashing the water from side to side as the drum turns.

I was supposed to get food for us. I was going to try the new Sainsbury's Local. It's always busy, and I've not nicked anything from there for a few weeks. The security guy was on to me last time, I'm sure, but the shop was packed, and I got away with it. I borrowed Andy's black baseball cap today, thinking I might not be recognised. It's getting harder, though.

As it was, I couldn't do it. I just had to get off the streets quickly after Emma saw me.

I wanted to talk to her – to tell her why I can't come back and explain why I left. She says she misses me, but I find that difficult to believe. I want her to understand why I ran away, though. If I hadn't I would have been arrested for taking Ollie. So how can I go back? It's hopeless.

I don't get why she's looking for me and why she says she wants me back. I don't know if I can trust her.

The only person I really trust is Andy, and I've let him down again. I'm always relying on him to feed me and I know it's not fair. I wouldn't have survived this long without him, though.

I met Andy a couple of months after I escaped – escaped from having to face my dad, the man who had betrayed me; escaped from the police, who were going to arrest me for everything I had done; escaped from the gang I had been living with for more than six years, who would kill me for grassing to the police – if they could find me. And escaped from Emma – the person who had done the least to hurt me, who I had hurt the most.

The weeks after I left felt like the worst of my life. They probably weren't; I've had my share of terrible times. But however bad things had been in the past I had always had a home – of sorts. When I walked away from my dad and Emma's house I had nowhere to go. No place where somebody would open the door and welcome me in – or even grunt an acknowledgement that I was actually there.

I made it to Stockport without too much bother – walking at night, keeping away from busy main roads as much as I could and finding some-where to hide out during the day. When it was really late – the early hours of the morning kind of late – I had to dodge into gardens to hide when I saw a car coming because I knew the police would stop me if they saw me out and about at that time. But I got quite good at it. During the day I would often hide in plain sight, hanging around where there were other kids or just going to a park, and I always managed to nick something to eat from somewhere. That was the easy bit.

The hard thing was being on my own. Even living with Rory and Donna Slater – the couple who had hidden me for more than six years after I was kidnapped – had been better than having nobody. Life there wasn't great, but there were other kids, and we helped each other. And I'd had Izzy – my friend. Thinking about her now makes me want to cry, but if I start, I won't stop.

Stockport was okay – there are some caves up above the town where loads of homeless are living. They tolerated me, but I don't think they liked me being around. I bet they were worried that if they were caught with a thirteen-year-old girl they would be accused of doing all sorts of stuff they hadn't done. So I told them I wanted to go to Manchester. I pretended to have friends here, and one of them said he'd help me – which was his way of getting rid of me, I suppose. I'm used to that now.

This bloke – Bartosz he was called – loved trains. He watched them all the time and he said there was a pattern to the times an inspector or guard or whatever they're called would board the local trains to do a ticket check. He told me which train to catch.

I was really scared, though. If I'd been caught, I'd have been done for. I bet there's pictures of me in all the police stations, because I'm a wanted criminal. I stole a *baby*. I picture a poster like the ones in old films – or maybe just like the one that Emma has produced.

The train was okay, though. I made it here to Manchester, although it wasn't much better than Stockport after all. I was still on my own.

I met Andy one day when the sun was shining. I remember that, because for once I felt warm. I'd just nicked some food from the express supermarket down in what I think of as the bottom end of Manchester. Where it joins on to Salford, I suppose. It was one of my favourite places, because the security guard was a fatty, and I knew I could run faster. But as I slid out of the door, hoping I hadn't been spotted but not really that bothered, I got the shock of my life. This young, fit, black guy was standing in Fatty's place, wearing a security uniform. He looked at my shocked face and knew exactly what I'd done. I set off running. I was quick and I dodged the people coming down the street – but he wasn't about to give up. Mostly these guys run for about ten metres to make a bit of a show and then turn round and go back, defeated once more by the dregs of Manchester. But this one was on a mission, and I was losing.

I raced across the road, down a side street and into some gardens I'd never seen before. People were out enjoying the sun and stared at me as I legged it over the grass and onto the path. He was getting closer.

Out of the corner of my eye, I saw a boy slouching on a bench, staring at a brightly coloured flowerbed in the centre where the paths met. It was so gaudy with its reds and yellows it hurt my eyes. The boy glanced at me as I ran past, and a couple of seconds later I heard a loud shout and a clatter.

'*Jesus*,' a deep voice yelled. 'You stupid kid – I nearly had him.'

I dodged behind some shrubs and stopped to grab my breath. The man might not have seen where I'd gone, and I thought that if I was lucky I might be safe – thanks to the boy. I was running out of steam – I hadn't eaten for two days.

I peered through the leaves and saw the boy on the floor, the big black guy sprawled on top of him. The guy pushed himself up and started brushing fiercely at his trousers with the pale palms of his black hands as he ripped into the kid for getting in the way.

The boy managed to wriggle into a kneeling position, and I could see blood on his face – where his cheekbone jutted out from his skinny cheek. It must have hurt. This kid probably weighed about the same as the black guy's left leg, and his jeans hung off him as if he'd borrowed them from an older brother.

'Sorry, mister,' he said, his voice weak and shaking. 'I didn't see you coming. I didn't mean to get in your way.' The boy looked petrified and the man stopped for a moment and looked at him properly.

'You're okay, kid. Sorry I shouted. I really wanted to catch that lad, though. It's my first day, and … Here, let me give you a pull up.' He held out his hand, and the boy took it. He tried to look at the blood on the boy's face, but the boy pushed his hand away.

I couldn't hear them any more, because two women had come to sit on a bench in front of my shrub, and they were yattering. The security guy looked my way once, brushed at his trousers again, said a couple of words to the boy and walked off – back towards his shop, where no doubt he would get a hot cup of tea and a bun for his efforts.

I looked at the treasure I had managed to nick. A sausage roll. It was still warm because I'd taken it from the hot cupboard, and now that the danger was past my mouth was watering. I decided to sit where I was, hidden under a bush that had huge pink flowers and shiny leaves but which was somehow quite empty underneath, almost like a kid's den.

The boy was walking along the path and would pass me soon. I should probably have thanked him, but I was scared of showing myself in case the man came back.

'You can come out, you know.' The voice was totally unlike the weak, scared version I had heard minutes earlier. There was some sort of accent too, but I didn't know enough to be able to recognise then that it was Scottish. He told me that later.

I stopped, the sausage roll halfway to my mouth, and stayed silent.

A face appeared between the leaves. 'Can you spare a wee bite for your rescuer?' He pushed his way through and sat down. 'Budge up,' he said.

I gave him half the sausage roll.

He was even skinnier that I had first thought. As he reached out his hand to take his share of the food I noticed the bone of his wrist sticking out like a golf ball, and his fingers were ridiculously long and white with torn, chewed nails.

I realised straight away how clever the boy was, though. Despite his scrawny build, I could tell there was nothing weak or shaky about this lad – voice or otherwise.

'What's your name?' he asked. 'I'm Andy.'

'Harry,' I said. He looked at me, his eyebrows raised, then took a bite of the sausage roll. 'Right you are. Harry it is, then.'

I've stopped thinking about how much I've let Andy down and how I'm going to make it up to him. Better to think of nothing, so I stare straight ahead and try to empty my mind of bad thoughts. My attempt at peace doesn't last long, though. I hear footsteps coming down the tunnel, walking quickly as if somebody knows exactly where they are going and tiny prickles of fear run up my arms. I've got nobody here to protect me.

I huddle down, pulling a blanket we found a couple of days ago around my shoulders. I tug the visor of Andy's cap down as far as I can. It might be that man again – the one who says there's a reward for finding me. But he's walking quickly – so if it's him, he knows where he's heading – straight to me.

The footsteps stop, right in front of me. But I don't look up.

'Hey, Harry – it's okay. It's only me. I got us some grub.'

Andy.

I let out my breath.

'It's fresh grub, too. I was dead lucky. Some guy had all his shopping in one of those free carrier bags and the handle broke. Everything ended up on the pavement – so I helped him pick it up. When he wasn't looking, I managed to grab a pack of sandwiches and shove 'em in my bag. I felt mean, though, 'cos he could see I was poor – probably homeless – and he gave me a quid for helping him. And I'd just nicked his bloody sandwich.'

It's typical of Andy to bring me half of everything he gets. He could have scoffed the lot, and I would never have known. But he wouldn't do that. It's like he needs to protect me, to look after me. It seems to make him happy for some reason, and it feels good to me.

We don't talk about the past. He pretends to believe I'm called Harry, even though everything he needs to know about me is printed on flyers lying all over the streets of Manchester, and Andy has got eyes. Even with my dark, cropped hair, my face is the same. I keep it dirty, and most people don't bother to look at me: scruffy urchin boy with a filthy neck – why would anybody look twice? Unless it's social services, and I can spot them a mile off. It's the shoes.

So he knows I'm a thirteen-year-old girl; that my name is Tasha Joseph; that I've run away from home. But it was never my home. Not really. And the flyers tell only a small part of the truth.

Andy passes me an old a plastic bottle filled with water from a tap in a public toilet.

'You okay now?' he asks.

I'd told him I wasn't feeling good and that's why I hadn't got any food. But I need to tell him the truth. It's not fair to lie.

'I'm sorry, Andy. I wasn't ill – I just felt awful 'cos I saw Emma.' He knows who Emma is; I told him her name last night. Everybody's seen her because she's always shouting about Tasha Joseph, about how she wants her to come home and how her baby brother is missing her. I don't believe it. She's lying.

Andy's gone quiet. Does that mean he's mad at me? I don't want him to leave me. I need him. He's opening the sandwich packet, and my belly feels like it's doing backflips.

Silently he hands me one of the two sandwiches and I take a huge mouthful.

I feel my nostrils flare and my mouth pulls down at the corners. It's an automatic reaction, and I think Andy will be cross with me because I'm ungrateful. But he just laughs.

'Sorry – not my choice,' he says with his mouth full. 'It's mingin'. That guy obviously has weird taste in sandwiches.'

'What is it?'

Andy passes me the packet. 'Falafel, spinach and tomato,' I read from the label. 'What the hell's a falafel?'

He just shrugs, and we both take another mouthful, wishing it was cheese, or tuna or something we've tasted before. But it's food.

We don't speak again until the sandwich has all gone, and I wait. I know he's got something to say.

'I saw Emma in town today too. I was looking for her.'

I stare at him. I'm confused. Why would he go looking for Emma?

'I wanted to hear what she had to say about the reward – the five thousand pounds that's being offered for you.'

I say nothing. Does he mean he was going to turn me in – take the full reward himself?

'Harry,' he says. 'Emma said nothing about no reward. She didn't mention it.'

'So?'

'So don't you think it's funny that if she's really offering a reward for you, she doesn't bother to mention it when she has a crowd of very likely customers for her money right in front of her? She offers cakes and all sorts if people will try to find you, but I asked around. She's never offered money.'

I look at Andy. He doesn't have to say it, but I know he will anyway.

'If Emma's not offering the money, and we know it's not the police because they just wouldn't, who the hell is it, Harry? Who wants to find you so bad that they're offering five bloody grand for you?'

I say nothing. I know the answer; I just refuse to say the name out loud.

5

'Emma, hi. It's Tom. Sorry it's taken me a while to get back to you.'

'Oh Tom, thanks so much for calling. I know how busy you are with work and stuff, so I'm sorry to bother you.'

Tom felt another pang of guilt.

'Did you hear the message – that I've seen Tasha?' Emma asked, the excitement shining in her voice. 'That means we know she's in Manchester – in the centre. That's good, isn't it? If we can narrow down the search it should be easier to find her, shouldn't it?'

'It certainly should be easier than not knowing which town she's in, yes.'

Before calling Emma, Tom had spent half an hour trying to come up with a strategy to deal with her expectations, but he had failed miserably. He felt doubly guilty because he should be seeing more of her now – at least, more of Ollie.

Three months after the trauma of Ollie being abducted, Emma had decided to have him christened. She had asked Tom to be Ollie's sole godparent, and he had been very happy to accept.

It was during the christening that she had asked if he could spare an hour after the other guests had left.

'I've got something to ask you, Tom, and please feel free to say no.'

Tom had been sure it was going to be something to do with Tasha, but he was wrong.

'I'm so pleased you agreed to be Ollie's godfather, but I can't help thinking about what would happen to him if I was ill or, worse case, if I died. He'd be an orphan. He couldn't go to my dad in Australia – his lifestyle would never suit a baby or a little boy, and there's nobody else in my family that I would consider to be a good parent.' Emma had paused and taken a sip of her wine as if she needed courage. 'But you *are* a good parent, Tom. I've seen you with Lucy, and you're so balanced. You let her think for herself, and try to guide her, but you never sound like a dictator.'

Tom interrupted.

'It's very kind of you to say these things about me, Emma. But they're not entirely true. I can be a grumpy bugger when I'm tired, so don't be under any illusion that I'm the perfect father. I'd love to be, if only I knew what that was.'

Emma laughed.

'I don't much believe in perfection. But I do believe in always trying to be the best we can, and I think that's what you're like. I'm serious, Tom. You're a good parent, and I respect your values.

That's why I'd like to ask if I can name you in my will as Ollie's guardian.'

Tom had been about to say something about Emma being ridiculous thinking about death at her age. But they were standing in her kitchen, on the very spot where her husband had been murdered – murdered because Emma had disobeyed the gang's instructions and informed the police of Ollie's kidnap. The gang – and in particular its enforcer, Finn McGuinness – hadn't liked that one little bit, and David had borne the brunt of their anger.

Flattered though Tom had been by Emma's suggestion that he be Ollie's guardian, he had put forward lots of arguments. His job had unpredictable hours; it was a long time since he'd looked after a baby; Ollie didn't know him that well.

'Sorry, Tom, but that's a daft argument. If he was put into foster care, he wouldn't know the people he was living with at all.'

In the end, Tom had admitted that he was honoured to be asked, and, although hoping it would never come to it, he would be delighted to be Ollie's guardian. Which was why he should be seeing more of the child, rather than staying away because of the inevitable arguments with Emma. Well, maybe not arguments – but heated discussions at least.

And now Emma had seen Tasha – which was wonderful news on many levels, but it would inevitably resurrect the same disagreements.

'Can you tell me exactly where you were when you saw Tasha, and precisely what happened?'

'I was on Market Street – the pedestrian bit – outside the Arndale. I was shouting out, telling her to come home. You know what I do, Tom – you've seen me. I said there would be cake for people who came to listen to me, and that guaranteed getting some of the homeless there. They're the people who'll know where she's hiding, I'm sure.' Emma paused and took a deep breath. 'Anyway, I looked up, and there was a kid – looked like a young boy – standing at the edge of the crowd. He was wearing a dirty-looking hoody and a black baseball cap. I couldn't see much hair, but what was poking out at the back looked dark, as though it had been cut with a pair of garden shears.'

'And you thought it was Tasha?'

'I *knew* it was Tasha. It was the eyes. When I'd got over the fact that she was there – listening to me – I leaped off the box and hurried towards her. I really thought she wanted to see me, Tom. That she wanted to come home. But she turned and fled, skipping round people walking in the opposite direction. She disappeared down one of the side roads and I couldn't catch her. I combed the streets for hours afterwards, hoping she'd taken refuge in some doorway that I'd missed or something. But she'd disappeared without a trace.' Emma took a deep breath. 'The important thing is that we know she's alive, Tom – and that she's not left Manchester. That's the best news I've had for months.'

'We're looking for her too, Emma, and it's a big help knowing she's somewhere close. We need her to help us put Finn McGuinness away for a long time. We won't make the kidnapping charge stick without her. We all know that Finn set up the abduction and coerced Tasha into stealing Ollie, but he was never seen with your baby.'

'But he had a gun, Tom – he threatened me.'

'Yes – he threatened you when you were in the car, but he didn't force you into the car at gunpoint. Look, Emma, I'm not trying to be clever here, but although we have a case against McGuinness, it would be a lot stronger if we had Tasha. I'm worried that because you're trying to get the whole world to find her, you're pushing her further underground, scared to come out in case she's recognised.'

There was silence at the other end of the line, and Tom could almost sense waves of indignation wafting his way. But he was right, and he'd been telling Emma this for months.

'All I care about, Tom, is getting Tasha home safely. If McGuinness doesn't get life, that's tough as long as Tasha is safe.'

Tom knew there was no arguing. He had tried before, but Emma was adamant.

She had seen for herself what a vindictive bastard Finn McGuinness was, but she seemed to be choosing to ignore it. If he was free, who knew what havoc he might decide to wreak on the lives of those responsible for his arrest. Tasha, for certain, wouldn't be safe.

If they could get the evidence to put him away permanently, they could finally rest easy in their beds.

6

I've been out again today. I'm not sure if it's safer to be out where there are hundreds of people walking around or better to stay below ground. If I'm out in the open, I think it's harder for somebody to grab me. People aren't always interested in what's happening around them, but I'm sure somebody would react if a kid was being dragged off the street. You'd hope so – but maybe not.

Andy gave me some money so I could phone Emma. He said we need to know for sure that she's not the one offering a reward for me because if it's not her, we need to start worrying. He still thinks there's a chance it is Emma, because he doesn't think she would announce such a vast amount of money to the world at large – five grand is wealth unimaginable to the poor of Manchester. People would kill for less – Rory Slater for one. He'd have topped somebody for a grand, I'm certain. Or worse still, he would have done it for nothing, just because Finn McGuinness told him to.

Andy thinks it's more likely that Emma might have chosen one or two people she thinks she can trust and given them the task of finding me in return for a reward.

I'm not sure about that, though.

I made it as far as the phone box and hung about outside. Just as I plucked up the courage to make the call, some guy shoved me out of the way and went in, piling up his money, turning to give me a sly, toothless grin.

I didn't call her. The loser who elbowed me gave me a good excuse. The truth is I'm scared of what Emma might say to me. I can't forget what I did, so how could she?

I decided I needed to tell Andy everything last night. I didn't want him to hate me, though, so before I told him the dreadful thing I'd done, I told him about how my dad had set up my abduction when I was six, how my mum died, and how I ended up living with Rory and Donna Slater.

'What was it like, living with a gangland family?' he asked me.

'I didn't realise for ages that they were part of a gang.' I answered. 'I thought it was normal to have to steal if you wanted to eat. We all did it, and because I didn't go to school, I didn't know any different. There was always a chance that one of the teachers would recognise me, see, so I stayed at home, and they put me to good use – everything from nicking stuff to weighing and measuring the drugs that Rory sold. The other kids that lived there were okay, really. I had a friend, but she died.'

Andy had looked at me with a frown when I said that. I didn't want to talk about Izzy, though. The thought of how she had been forced to spend the last few weeks of her life, and what my life might have become, still gives me nightmares. I didn't want Andy to know that I had agreed to kidnap my baby brother to save myself from a life as a thirteen-year-old prostitute, being pawed over by fat, greasy guys who got their kicks from screwing kids. I could sometimes feel their grubby hands touching my body while I slept, and I couldn't stand the thought of Andy imagining me like that.

'When did you realise – about the gang, I mean?'

'When I first met Finn McGuinness. I heard him talking to Rory, and I knew Rory was being made to do stuff – that he wasn't in charge, like I'd always thought. But even Finn wasn't top dog. There was somebody higher up. Finn and Rory were just part of his operation. I don't know who the main guy was, though.'

'So why do you think the police are looking for you now?'

We both knew Emma wasn't the only one asking about me, and although I tried to pretend the police are looking because I'm a runaway, that isn't very convincing given the number of other kids there are on the streets. Why single me out for special treatment?

'They want me because of what I did.' I said it out loud; I admitted I had done something terrible. And I knew I would have to tell Andy the rest.

He waited. He was good like that. So I told him I had stolen Ollie – my cute, lovable, baby half-brother – that I had walked out of the house with him, and handed him over to Rory. I just stuck to the facts; I kept to myself the way I had felt, but the memories came flooding back.

At first, the planning had felt good. I wanted to punish my dad for betraying me and for setting up the abduction that had killed my mother all those years earlier. But Ollie had made me feel soft inside, and I wasn't expecting that. I kept telling myself to stop being weak, that my dad deserved the pain and that I had to save myself from the alternative life I knew was my only other option.

Walking out of the house with Ollie had been easy. I had felt quite clever for a moment. But when I picked his warm little body out of his pushchair and held him out to Rory – a man who stank of stale booze and cigarettes – I had felt sick. Ollie had turned back to me, stretched out his arms towards me, wanting me to take him back from the horrible man who was squeezing him too tight. He had looked frightened, his eyes wide and his mouth open, ready to scream. Rory had put his hand over Ollie's mouth and I'd shouted then. 'Don't hurt him,' I had cried. 'He's just a baby.'

At that moment I had wanted more than any-thing to take Ollie back – to pluck his chubby body in its cuddly down romper suit from Rory's arms and run as fast as I could.

But I didn't tell Andy any of this. I only told him what I had done.

He stared at me with his mouth open like a goldfish. I had to carry on. I didn't want to make it sound less than it was: evil, mean, destructive. I had thought then that it was the only thing I could do, but how could I explain this to a kind, thoughtful boy like Andy? That Finn had given me no choice? That he had planned it and made it clear what my options were?

I rushed to finish my story, swallowing my words as they spilled out, telling him stuff I hadn't wanted him to know, but feeling I had to somehow make excuses for myself.

'Finn told me if I didn't take Ollie, I would have to go to Julie's, the place my friend Izzy – the one who killed herself – escaped from. It wasn't a good place, Andy. Anyway, I hated my dad. I still do, for what he did. I wanted to make him suffer.'

But never Ollie, I thought to myself. It should never have been Ollie. My baby brother.

Andy was quiet for a moment, thinking. He picked up a pebble and threw it up and down in the air, catching it and tossing it up again, as if he was weighing everything up.

'So why does Emma want you back, do you think, if you stole her bairn?'

'I don't know. It doesn't make sense to me. That's why I had to leave. The police would have arrested me, Emma hated me, my dad was a useless piece of crap – and I couldn't go back to Rory because I'd grassed on him and the rest of them. He'd have killed me. What else could I have done? So I came here.'

'What happened to Rory and Finn, then?' Andy asked.

I didn't know the answer. I'd been trying to find out – to track down some of the other kids from the Slaters' house. I'd hung around their school for a while at the beginning, hiding in the door of a derelict house that had obviously been the victim of a fire, because everything I touched turned my fingers black. But none of the kids ever came. They must have been taken somewhere else. I didn't know if Rory had done a runner with the lot of them, or been locked up for keeping me hidden all those years and a whole string of other crimes they might have uncovered.

That policeman – Tom, Emma called him – knew what Rory had done to me, and he didn't look like the kind of bloke who would let him get away with it.

'I think the cops might have arrested Rory, but I don't know about Finn. It doesn't matter much. Whether Finn is inside or not, he's got contacts. He knows I grassed them up – and he'll get me if that's what he wants. I've been expecting something to happen since the moment I ran.'

It seems far more likely that Finn McGuinness is offering the reward. Why he's waited so long is a mystery, but it would be just like him to offer money to some young guy who in the end will probably never see a penny of it. But I still want to know for sure. I want to know where the danger is coming from. I should have made that call.

I feel safer now that I'm back underground. I don't want Andy to hate me after everything I told him and I wonder what he's thinking. He's been so good to me, and I don't want to spoil things. I plucked up the courage last night to ask him why he looked out for me all the time. He said it felt good to be able to protect somebody, then he clammed up. I'm going to try to explain better about what my life was like. I'll tell him about the Pit, how it felt to be thrown into a damp, cold, dark hole in the ground for not doing as I was told, and how it felt to learn my dad had sold my young life to save his own skin.

I wander back through the tunnel, back to Andy, and I realise that after I've told him the rest I'm going to have to leave him and move on. I'm a danger to anybody around me, and I don't want Andy to get dragged into my mess. My eyes mist over at the thought of losing him, and my step falters. Nobody looks at me as I walk past.

There's something funny about the atmosphere down here tonight. Everybody seems jumpy – or is it just me? Tension seems to be bouncing off the walls. I'm looking at the floor as I walk, making sure I don't tread in anything nasty, but out of the corner of my eye I notice that nobody is looking at me because they're all looking away, down the tunnel towards our pitch.

I lift my eyes from the floor and stop dead. Quietly I move to the side of the tunnel, deep into the shadows.

Andy is up ahead, and the man from the other night is with him. I know it's him – it's the way he stands; the slight bow in his legs with his feet spread apart. He's got a knife – against Andy's throat. I edge a little closer so I can hear what's being said. The tunnel echoes and the voice sounds weird, but I can make out the words.

'You know something, don't you, kid?'

Andy starts to shake his head, then obviously thinks better of it with the knife up against his neck.

'No – why do you think that?'

'Because when I came asking the other night, you were too fucking interested. That's why.'

'Only 'cos you mentioned five grand. I'd do anything for a piece of that.' Andy sounds convincing, but his voice is shaking.

'There's people looking for this girl – serious people – people who would slit your throat and not even think about it. Just like I'm going to.'

I'm about to jump out of the shadows and give myself up. He can't kill Andy – this is my problem. Then he carries on speaking, so I stay where I am.

'But not yet,' he says. 'I think you know something.' He pushes his knife against Andy's throat, forcing his chin up. 'Look at me, kid.' Andy opens his eyes and stares at the man. Even from here I can imagine the terror in those eyes. Andy's a peace-loving kid, and I think he's known too much violence in his short life. Haven't we all, I guess.

The guy is talking again, pushing the knife harder, and I can see darker marks around the blade. It can only be blood.

'If I find out you're hiding something from me – you're dead. Tell me where she is, I'll let you live. Have you got that?'

Andy can't nod without his neck being sliced open, so he whispers, 'Yes.'

'And just so that you know I'm not kidding …' The man pulls the knife away but grabs Andy's hair in his other hand and pulls him down over his extended leg and lets go. Andy falls hard onto the floor, and I hear the crack of his head as he fails to protect it with his bad arm. He is sprawled on the floor, unable to move.

The man pulls back his skinny shin and kicks Andy in the guts. Andy cries out once, and the man laughs.

'Pathetic. If you think that's hurting, you ain't got a clue what's coming.'

He is still laughing as he walks away, hands pushed deep into the pockets of his puffa jacket.

I wait until I'm sure he's gone. I don't know if he's going to come back or not, but I can't leave Andy like this. He's not moving, and I don't know how badly he's hurt.

This is all my fault. Again. Why is it that I bring misery everywhere I go? I don't mean to, but it just seems to happen.

I know that I'm going to have to move on – leave Andy and walk away from the feeling of being safe when I'm with him. I need to be on my own, just as I thought, where I can't destroy anybody else's life. Maybe I should just give in and let them have me. Then nobody would have to worry about me any more.

7

'Hello,' Emma said, slightly out of breath after running from Ollie's room to her own bedroom. She could have let the call go to answerphone, but she was obsessive about answering phone calls – just in case.

There was silence at the other end of the line, and Emma felt her hopes rise. Could it be …?

'Hello – is that you, Tasha?' she asked.

She heard a chuckle down the phone that sounded more derisive than amused.

'Were you expecting to hear from her, Mrs Joseph?' The voice was male, but young. And even down the phone line she could sense the poison.

Emma said nothing. She waited, wanting to put the phone down, but if this was about Tasha, she couldn't.

'You want to cut me off, don't you – but I know you can't. Because perhaps I know something about Tasha – maybe I can tell you where she is. Is that what you're thinking, Emma?' There was something slick about his tone that made Emma shudder.

'I'm not thinking anything,' she said, trying to sound brisk and efficient.

'Well, let me explain something to you, shall I? Tasha's been a bad girl. She's upset a lot of very important people.'

Emma made a pfff sound – she couldn't help herself.

'Oh no, I wouldn't go dissing these guys. I thought you, more than anybody, would know better than that. I have a feeling you've seen what they're capable of. But they've got long memories, so don't underestimate them.'

'What do you want?'

'I want to know where Tasha is.' The voice had become hard, the speech faster. Less of the slippery innuendo – he was getting to the point.

'I don't know where she is, and if you knew anything at all, you would know that I'm looking for her too.'

'And you think we don't know that? The police are looking as well, and we both know why. They want her to give evidence against Finn McGuinness.'

'They don't need Tasha for that. They have a cast iron case.' Emma knew this wasn't true, but maybe they didn't.

She was wrong. Another of those chuckles made her skin erupt in goosebumps.

'They need her. But it's not going to happen, Emma. If you find her, we'll know. She was one of us – and that makes her betrayal the worst kind. We're happy for you to carry on looking, though. Because we're watching you, you see. If you don't want to risk your little boy's life again, you need to help us find her.' The threat to Ollie dripped like ice water down her spine, but the caller hadn't finished. 'You owe her nothing. Because of her you nearly lost your baby, and your husband died. All because of Tasha.' The last four words were uttered in a slow, sing-song voice, but they drove the fear from Emma's heart.

'You're wrong about Tasha. My husband died because of his own mistakes. Ollie was taken because of what *he* did. None of this should have happened to Tasha. And you had better believe this. If I find her first, you will never get to her. You need to understand that.'

She replaced the receiver.

Her anger lasted seconds. Long enough to get her through that last sentence, but that was all. Her legs felt weak, and her breathing was rapid. She made her way slowly to the bed and sat down, reaching out a hand behind to steady herself.

Had that been a really stupid thing to do? Would they come for her, now – or try to take Ollie again?

Why now, though? Why wait so long for all of this? It was months since it all happened.

Emma decided to give herself five minutes to calm down, then she would go and check that Ollie had settled. Then she was going to call Tom.

Keep calm, she told herself.

A few minutes later she felt ready to move and was pushing herself up from the bed when the phone started to ring again.

Emma hesitated. Should she answer it or not?

She had to. She reached out and picked it up.

'Hello,' she said softly, not knowing what to expect. Silence. It was him again.

'Now listen,' she said, her voice strong and determined. 'Don't call me again with your threats. I don't want to know what you think – okay?'

'Emma?' A quiet, light voice whispered down the line. Emma held her breath for just a second.

'Oh God – it's you, isn't it? Tasha? Is it you, darling?' Emma felt tears spring to her eyes. 'Oh, Tasha – come home, sweetheart. Please. Let me come and get you. Where are you?'

She knew she was gabbling, but she had waited months for this moment. She had to give the child chance to speak, though.

'Are you offering a reward to find me?'

'What?'

'Is it you? I just need to know. It's causing too much trouble. People will kill each other for a share.' The voice was pleading, nearly crying. Tasha was tough – this wasn't like her.

'Tasha – I would give anything to have you back, but I didn't think money would help, darling. I'm not offering anything at all, except cakes and sandwiches. Why would you think that?'

'Is it my dad? No – don't answer that. He never wanted me back anyway.'

Emma took a moment before replying. Of course Tasha didn't know that David was dead. How could she tell her? She had no idea whether Tasha would be devastated or pleased, but telling her like this, over the phone, wasn't the way to do it.

'Sweetheart, about your dad ...'

But Tasha wasn't listening.

'Is it Tom – is he offering money?'

'No. He would have told me. He wants to see you, though.'

Emma heard a mirthless laugh.

'Of course he does. I *know* what I did. I *know* I'm a criminal. I *know* you want me back to make me suffer for everything I've done. But don't offer money. Don't keep looking for me. You're helping the wrong people.'

'Tasha – you've got it all wrong. I ...'

'Goodbye, Emma.' The phone went dead.

'Shit,' Emma hissed. She quickly dialled one four seven one and got the number of the phone box. She called it immediately, and waited.

With relief she heard the tone change as the phone was picked up.

'Tasha?' she called.

'Uh? This is a phone box. Nobody here except me, and I'm waiting for a call. Get off the line.' The gruff voice sounded angry.

'Is there a young teenage girl there, close to the box?' she asked.

'There ain't nobody but me. I told you. Now get off the bloody line.' The phone went dead.

Emma dropped the handset, sat down on the bed again and put her head in her hands.

Tasha knew the police were looking for her, but had completely misinterpreted the reason. And how could she believe that Emma wanted to do her any harm? It made sense, though. If she had been brought up the way Tasha had, she would probably have believed the same thing.

For eight months Emma had been waiting for that call, and when at last it had happened, she'd got it wrong. What should she have said? What could she have done to make it go better? Had she finally lost Tasha for good?

8

'Thanks for the money, Andy,' I whisper as I crouch down next to where he is sitting. After we had checked out Andy's injuries, he had insisted I make the call.

He doesn't ask what happened on the phone. He'll wait until I'm ready to tell him.

'We're a team,' is all he has to say.

That makes it harder. I know he's going to be mad at me for leaving, but I can't stay with him. He's taken a kicking for me, and not many people in my life have ever done that, so now I have to do the right thing. I could wait until he's out to do this, but then I know he would come looking for me – just one more person trying to find me. Anyway, I owe him.

Moving home doesn't take much effort when all you have is a couple of sheets of cardboard for bedding and a plastic bag with a few extra clothes, and I start to gather my things together. I'll have to leave the fire can. That's Andy's.

'What're you doing?' he asks quietly, watching me.

'I'm going.' There's not much else I can say, really.

'What – back to Emma's?' he says, a mixture of hope for me and sadness for himself making his face pull in different ways – the mouth smiling, the eyes looking scared.

I should say yes. That would be the end of it. But I don't want to lie to him.

'I think I'm better on my own, that's all.'

'That's crap, and you know it,' he says. 'You're right that you need to go, but I'm coming with you. I'm not staying here to get my bollocks kicked again, thanks, so where are we off to?'

I know I should say no, but I can't. I tell him about an old warehouse I've heard of down by the river. There used to be shops and all sorts down there, but now it's all bricked up. Well – it was until somebody un-bricked a bit of it.

'Sounds perfect,' he says, bending down to pick up his bits, including the fire can. 'Let's go then.'

The new place is about half a mile from our last pitch, and we find ourselves a space that's not too close to the other groups that live here. We don't trust anybody now, but nobody bothers us or seems to mind us being here.

This is a proper building, not just a tunnel, so I thought it would be warmer, but the roof is high up and full of holes, and the windows have long since gone, so it's every bit as cold. It doesn't echo like the tunnel did. The sounds are more muffled, and I sit still and listen to the noises around me. There's no dripping water, but an old wooden window frame is loose and is banging in the wind.

'Do you want to tell me how things went on the phone with Emma?' Andy says as he starts to make the fire. 'Doesn't matter if you don't.'

Andy had kept the pound coin the guy had given him for picking up his shopping and nicking his butties. He'd been saving it for something special, and he had said phoning Emma was special. Now that the call was done, I pushed what was left of his money into his hand.

'Those phone boxes don't always cough up the change, so I went into a shop for some 10p pieces. I didn't want to lose 40p of your money.'

40 p was 40p. It was enough to buy us an everyday value loaf of bread from the supermarket, and that would keep us going for days. But it's Andy's to spend as he wants.

'What did Emma say?' he asks, keeping his voice soft. We're new here, and so we need to keep a low profile for a bit, just till we're sure we're accepted. 'Come on, Harry – how did it go?'

It's my turn to shrug. He says I don't have to tell him, but he paid for the call in more ways than one, so it's only fair really.

'She says she's not offering a reward. Neither are the police.'

I think we both knew this before I made the call. I just wanted to be sure. I know who it is – I've always known. I just thought they would have come for me before now.

'Emma says she wants me to go home – it was all "darling" and "sweetheart" – but that can't be right, can it? She can't possibly want me anywhere near her or Ollie.'

'Harry, have you ever thought she might actually mean it? Maybe she gets you?'

I laugh at that. She certainly did not get me. Not one little bit. When I moved in with her and my dad I hardly spoke, and when I did I was rude. I could tell it annoyed Emma. She was okay with me when everything was going mental, but that was because she wanted her baby back, and I was her best bet.

'Andy, Emma is a nice lady. She has nice manners and she's kind to people. I'm a kid who has nicked from every supermarket in west Manchester, carried skunk in my backpack on trains … And my greatest stunt? I stole her bloody baby. So sure, she's bound to want me back.'

Andy pokes our sad little fire with a piece of wood that was ultimately going to end up in the can with the others.

'So why spend all this time and effort looking for you? I think you're wrong; I think she means it.'

'Well, that's a lovely thought, but the police would arrest me if I went back – so it's a no-brainer. Let's forget Emma and try to work out what we're going to do about that nasty bastard who's trying to find me.'

I don't know why I suggest this, though – because neither of us is going to come up with an answer. There isn't one. He'll either find me or he won't.

9

The kitchen was filled with the delicious aroma of a Tuscan beef stew that was simmering in the oven, the tomatoes, spices and red wine combining to create a smell that always made Emma think of cold, winter evenings in front of a warm fire. But tonight she wasn't cooking it for herself. She couldn't bear the thought of food. It was for Tom. She needed him, and the least she could do in return for his help was cook his dinner.

She paced the kitchen, waiting for him to arrive, conscious she shouldn't always rely on him, but not knowing what else to do.

The doorbell rang, and she rushed to let him in.

'Tom, thank you so much for coming. I feel guilty for calling you, but I've nobody to talk to who understands this whole mess except you.'

They were both silent for a moment as they thought of the men she should have been able to rely on, both of whom had let her down in different ways and who were now gone from her life. Except Emma wasn't entirely sure that one of them had gone completely.

After nearly eight years of agonising over the sudden break-up of her relationship with her ex-fiancé, Jack, she finally understood why he'd had to leave when he did, and why he now had to stay below the radar. But although she had never told Tom, Emma suspected Jack was spooking around in her computer. A brilliant hacker and computer security expert, he had always been able to take control of her computer remotely and make it do unexpected things. It used to amuse her, but now she just wished he would make himself known so she could talk to him. She had taken to using sticky note software to leave subtle messages on her desktop that only Jack would understand. He could read them from afar and know that she still loved him. And she was sure he *was* reading them, because he always moved the notes a few pixels to the right. It was his way of letting her know he was there.

It was a secret that Emma kept to herself. It wouldn't have been fair to tell Tom, who was suffering as much as she was at the loss of his brother for a second time.

Tom was busy taking his Barbour off. It was dripping with rain, and he shook it in the porch before hanging it on a hook. Emma couldn't help thinking that although he was Jack's brother Tom was nothing like him. Both men were tall, but Tom had broad shoulders whereas Jack was leaner, more intense, and until the last time she saw him Jack had always had long, almost black, bushy hair that he tied back in a ponytail when he was forced to look smart. Tom had dark-blond hair that he kept short and a bit spiky. They were chalk and cheese, but she had sometimes wished Jack had a bit more of Tom's solidity.

He stepped into the hall and gave her a hug.

'It's good to see you, and don't ever feel guilty about calling me. I want to help. I know I don't always say what you want to hear, and that makes it difficult for me sometimes. But I won't lie to you.'

'I know. Look, come through to the kitchen, have a glass of wine, and I'll tell you what's happened today.'

'Okay, but first – where's my godson? Is he in bed?'

'Sorry, he is. I had to put him down, because if he'd stayed up it would have taken me forever to get him to sleep. He'd have been so excited. You can pop up and see him, if you like.'

Tom grinned at her and took the stairs two at a time. Ollie asleep was a perfect picture. On his back, arms above his head, blankets kicked off and legs splayed, he looked like a starfish – and one with the cutest face.

Emma made her way into the kitchen, poured two glasses of red wine and leaned against the units, trying to decide what to say to Tom – what to tell him, and in what order. She had been going round and round the options, but in the end there was only one thing for it.

'Tasha called me.' The words burst out of her before Tom was even through the kitchen door.

He stopped dead, as if he hadn't heard her right. 'You're joking?'

Emma nodded and took a gulp of her wine.

'She wanted to know if I was offering a reward for her.'

'What? You're not, are you? Please tell me you haven't offered half the homeless of Manchester money for turning her in.'

'No, of course I haven't.' She pointed to the glass of wine sitting on the central unit. 'I'm not completely insane. That would cause a riot. But it seems somebody is offering money to find her, and I'm fairly sure it's not you.'

'No, it's not, although we could really do with finding her.'

Tom picked up his wine, and Emma could tell from his face that he was weighing his words.

'Spit it out, Tom. What are you thinking?'

'If it's not you, and it's not me, there's only one other person who has anything to gain by finding Tasha.'

The name McGuinness hung in the air between them, unspoken.

'Why now, though? He's had months to look for her, and it's the first we've heard about this reward.'

Tom looked uncomfortable.

'I told you weeks ago that McGuinness was ill and that's why his court case had been delayed, but I didn't tell you how ill because I know you want him to suffer for everything he's done. I guessed you would think dying in his sleep would have been too good for him.'

'Absolutely. He deserves to rot in prison for a long time.'

Tom nodded, as if that was what he had expected from her. 'A few days after he was charged, McGuinness was beaten up. We don't know who by – nobody's saying. He was being held on remand in Manchester Prison – Strangeways, as it used to be – and somebody got to him, probably from a rival gang. He was thumped with some force in his stomach and ended up with peritonitis.'

Tom took a sip of his wine. 'He went on to suffer septic shock and he was in intensive care for weeks. He wasn't fit for visitors for a long time, so he wouldn't have had a chance to put the word out. We didn't think he was going to survive, to tell you the truth, but I didn't want you to know. He's recovered – and I guess he knows he's going down. But with Tasha's evidence, his sentence will be considerably worse. It's only recently that he's been in a position to focus on finding her, and silencing her.'

Emma felt the weight of it all settling on her like a heavy stone. She wanted it to be over so they could put it behind them, where it belonged. Part of a life that was done, parcelled up and stored, so that they could move ahead without any burden dragging them down. And for her, that would only work if she got Tasha back too.

'Surely there are others who can give evidence against him? Do you really need Tasha?'

'There are plenty of people that could. But they won't. We caught several members of the gang that night. but none of them would risk going against their enforcer. They know they'd be dead within hours. McGuinness has enough contacts outside to see to that. Rory Slater is petrified of saying a word about anything in case he gives something away that gets him killed. It's amazing to watch some of these tough guys crumble when they think somebody bigger and uglier can get to them.'

'What about his wife, or can't she be forced to give evidence?'

'We can't compel her. She's already been found guilty of so many crimes – don't forget the under-aged prostitution on top of Ollie's kidnap. She's been given a hefty prison sentence, which is likely to be longer than Finn's as things stand. That's why we have to find Tasha.'

Emma shook her head in disgust at the McGuinness pair and started to get plates and cutlery ready.

'What else did Tasha say?' Tom asked. 'Did you manage to persuade her to come home?'

Emma laughed, but without a trace of amusement.

'She thinks you're going to arrest her. I don't think she has any idea what's happened at all. She asked if David was putting up the reward, but she discounted that fairly quickly based on his previous performance. She obviously doesn't know he's dead, and I didn't want to tell her on the phone.'

Emma's sadness for Tasha was reflected in Tom's expression.

'Was there anything she said that would help us find her? Where was she calling from?'

Emma handed over a piece of paper with the call box number on. 'She won't have used a phone close to where she's living, though. She's too smart for that. At least we know she's in Manchester – and somewhere fairly central – but I know that's a lot of ground to cover.'

Tom texted the phone number through to Becky to pass to the team looking for Tasha.

'She thinks the reward that's being offered is putting her in danger,' Emma said as she put a plate of hot food in front of Tom.

'She's probably right – but if the reward has come from McGuinness she's already in danger. If she calls again, you have to make her understand that. We can try making it known on the streets that she's not in any trouble with the police, but I don't know if she'll believe that.'

Emma debated whether to tell him the rest. If, by drawing attention to Tasha, she was really putting the girl in danger, she needed to know what to do. She took a mouthful of the stew, barely tasting it, and chewed for a moment.

'Tasha's wasn't the only call I received.'

Tom continued to eat, but he raised his eyes to hers, and she could see he was listening to every word as she recounted the threats made by the young-sounding man on the phone.

'But it's just words, Tom,' she concluded. 'If Tasha gets back to us, we can make sure she's safe, can't we?'

Tom put down his fork.

'And how, precisely, do you think we're going to do that, Emma? You know what happened here, in this very kitchen.'

Emma was shocked that he would mention it. Did he think she ever forgot that her husband had died on her kitchen floor, beaten to a pulp by Finn McGuinness's men?

'Don't look like that,' he said. 'I'm being tough because *you've* got to be tough. We could make this place like Fort Knox, but you've got to go out some time. If for any reason Tasha comes back, you call me. Don't wait – not even for five minutes. Have you got that, Emma, because this isn't a game. You're not only putting yourself and Tasha in danger. There's Ollie too.'

Emma had been so sure it would all be fine and that they just needed Tasha to come home. She pushed the food away from her, the dark red sauce of the stew suddenly looking like nothing more than a pool of blood.

10

With each day that passes, I've been starting to feel more frightened. I thought it would work the other way round – that each day nobody comes looking for me, I'll get more confident. It hasn't worked like that. It's three days since I phoned Emma. The lump on Andy's head has gone down, and we're getting used to our new home. I think I like it better than the tunnel, although there are more rats, and I don't like them much.

Andy went out today on what he called a special mission. I don't like him going out alone. I'm terrified that something will happen to him, or that he'll realise that I'm a danger to him and move off somewhere else. He was gone all day, but he's back now, thank goodness. I want to ask him where he's been, but I don't really have the right to do that. I learned a long time ago never to ask questions.

'What are you looking at me like that for?' he asks, and then he smiles. 'Ah – I get it. You thought I was going to run out on you, didn't you?'

I don't answer.

'Don't be so bloody soft, Harry. That's not going to happen. But there's always a chance that something might go wrong – like it nearly did the other night. Kids like me get beaten up all the time – and if that happens, you're going to have to get yourself to somewhere safe. You can't cope on your own.'

My chin goes up and my lips tighten. It's what Rory used to call my obstinate face, just before he slapped the expression off it.

Andy pushes an old, used brown envelope into my hands.

'This is for you,' he says. 'Put it somewhere really safe – where nobody will look. Okay?'

I hold the envelope out and start to open it.

'No, don't look,' he says. 'Not until you need to.'

I don't know what he means.

'It's your escape fund,' he tells me. 'If anything bad happens and you need to get away, you've got to go to Emma, whether you like it or not. I'm going to try to keep you safe, but if I screw up, this is everything you'll need to get to her.'

I feel my mouth drop open and I don't know what to say. So I say nothing and fight hard not to cry. I don't know why he is so good to me – I'm sure I don't deserve it.

Andy looks down at his hands, giving me a moment. He chooses to talk over my confusion.

'I've read the stuff on those flyers. I've listened to Emma. I don't think she would bring her wee bairn out to try to find you unless she really cares. She wants you to go home to her, and I'm thinking you should.'

'I'm not leaving you, Andy. So you can forget it.'
I try to give him back the envelope.

'Let's just say that if I'm not around – and I'm
not going to walk out on you, so don't go pulling
that face – but if you're on your own for any reason
you have to promise me that you'll go to Emma.'

He can see me looking at him, my face scrunched
up in a puzzled frown. He looks down at the ground,
and I can't see his eyes.

'I haven't always got things right in the past,' he
says. 'I need to get it right this time – with you.' He
looks up – straight at me. 'Don't ask me to explain.'

I don't know what to say but I know I can't force
him to tell me. I want to believe he's right about
Emma, though – that she really does want me back.
But for the moment I don't have to decide because
I've still got Andy.

'I know where Emma lives now,' Andy says, as if
his last words had never been spoken. 'I've worked
out a couple of different ways you can get there
when you need to. It's all in the envelope – trains,
buses, a bit of cash for the fares and that. Couldn't
run to a taxi.' He looks up with a sideways grin.

I'm still staring at the envelope.

'Put it away, now. Stick it down your pants or
something.'

I don't ask where he's got the money from,
because I know.

When we were first together we agreed we would
never beg in the streets. I wouldn't do it because I
didn't want to be recognised, but Andy wouldn't do

it because he was ashamed. Ashamed of the life he had never wanted to live; ashamed of the person he had become – stealing to eat, sheltering in damp, miserable tunnels. I don't know much, but I do know that this isn't the life he wants.

I know he won't have nicked the money. That isn't his thing. We only ever steal what we need – enough to keep us alive. So he must have begged, and I know exactly what he would have done. He would have rolled up his sleeves, so that people could see his deformed arm, and he would have held it so that it looked even worse. He knew how to dislocate his shoulder – he said it was because it had been done so many times that it popped in and out easy as anything – and it made his arm hang at a really odd angle. He would have sat outside the posh shops, looking like a pathetic, skinny, injured kid so people would feel sorry for him. I know how much he hates pity, but he's done it for me.

I want to kiss him, but I know he wouldn't like that. At least, I don't think he would.

'Now,' he says. 'I'm going to have to own up to saving some of the money for a special treat tonight.'

He looks at me, and he makes me wait.

'We're going to have chips!'

I can't speak because I can taste the chips, dripping with vinegar and loads of salt. I bet we can get some free ketchup too – perhaps take a few extra sachets to put on sandwiches – especially if we end up with those falafel things again. My mouth is watering.

'Where are we going?' I ask.

'We're going to go up the back way, stick to the alleys as far as we can. We'll have to come out when we get to Cross Street, but it will be busy if we time it right. There's something on at the theatre, and there were loads of people around earlier. If we wait until they all come out, they'll be milling around going to restaurants and stuff. Best place to hide is in a crowd.'

I'm not sure if I can wait that long, but for a treat like a bag of chips between us I can ignore the angry noises my belly is making.

It was worth the wait.

We barely make it out of the shop before we're digging into the chips, each of us making sure that in our excitement we don't take more than the other is getting. We walk back towards Albert Square, heads down over the shared packet, hoovering up every last morsel. The guy in the shop gave us some scraps too, so we're in heaven.

When we've finished we dodge down some of the quieter streets and make our way back to our pitch, our bellies for once feeling full. The empty chip paper gets thrown in the first bin we see, but only after I've licked the salty, vinegary mess off it.

Once we get off the main road and there's nobody else about, Andy starts mimicking some of the posh people in the chippy who had behaved as if going into a place like that was a special treat – an experience to share with their friends as they tried to live like normal people. I tell Andy that I bet they take the chips home to eat off a plate, rather than be seen eating from a bag in the street. By then, the chips will be cold, pale and soggy. What a waste.

He carries on messing about, making me smile, and I run on ahead a bit, pretending I want nothing to do with him. He's doing a posh person walk and shouting something silly about chipped potatoes. I pretend to ignore him for a minute then, laughing, I spin round to say something funny about the 'bat-taar' on the fish, but the words freeze in my throat.

The end of the alley is lit by the bright lights of central Manchester, but a dark shadow is standing at the entrance, top heavy, bowed legs planted firmly apart, arms slightly lifted from his side. I know the shape. I recognise it.

'Andy!' I scream. For a moment I'm frozen to the spot, terrified of what might be about to happen. But Andy's in danger, and within seconds I'm running back towards him.

He swivels his neck to look behind him and he sees the man too. He's a lot closer than I am. He spins back towards me.

'Run – Tasha – run,' he shouts. It's the first time he has ever called me by my name.

I don't want to run – I don't want to leave him.

'Go,' he yells.

I hesitate for just a second, and the man rushes towards Andy, arms out to push him over. It's not Andy he wants, it's me.

But Andy's having none of it. He moves into the middle of the unlit alley, his skinny frame looking frail and defenceless in the shadows. He's not going to let the guy get past, and I know he wants me to escape.

I turn and run as fast as I can, down the alley and into the pedestrian street beyond. There's a car park just off the street, and I sneak in and crouch down between the cars, watching and waiting for the man to come out of the alley after me, hoping that Andy has just slowed him down a bit and maybe got knocked over into the bargain.

I think I hear a scream, but I don't know where it's coming from. The alley? Manchester's noisy at this time of night, and it might be someone screaming with laughter. A lot of girls seem to scream for no reason that I can see. Please God, don't let it be Andy. Don't let him be hurt.

I know that's wishful thinking.

The minutes pass, time dragging. I'm just beginning to think that the man has gone back the way he came when he appears from the alley and stands still, weighing up the scene. He's not given up on me, but he can't see me where I'm hiding, and a few people give him an odd look. I can see he's covered in something. Something dark. I know it must be blood, and hope it's his, from a busted nose, or something.

Andy.

The man looks around a bit, but he looks like he's getting worried about the attention, so he clears off, trying to look as if he hasn't got a care in the world. I wait just seconds. I need to get to Andy.

I leap up from behind the car and set off at a run, back down the alley. I can't see him anywhere. Perhaps he's escaped.

Then I see a foot sticking out from the back doorway of an old building. I don't have to guess twice as I sprint up the alley.

'Andy!' I scream, falling to my knees by his side. His hands are holding his stomach, and he's bleeding – the warm, sticky blood oozing between his fingers. He's been stabbed. I touch his belly, feeling the hot, sticky fluid, and whisper his name, stroking his hair, getting blood on his face.

He can't hear me. I kiss his cheeks, his forehead, his lips, and I cry, my tears mingling with the blood.

His eyes flutter open, and he tries to smile. He's not dead, but I know he soon will be.

'Stay there,' I say foolishly. 'I'm going to get help.'

I rush out onto the main road, shouting for help.

'Please – somebody help me. There's a boy injured down here. Call an ambulance.'

One or two people look at me, but most hurry by, giving me a wide berth. A filthy kid, now covered in blood, asking for help? Not on your life, I can hear them thinking.

I need to act quickly.

A man and his wife are walking towards me, arms linked, laughing about something. They're having a great time, and I'm about to ruin their evening.

She's swinging an expensive-looking handbag from one hand. I wait for them to get close, and then I charge the woman, ripping the handbag from her arm.

She screams, and the man shouts. I'm sure he will chase me – he has to, or it will have been for nothing – but just to make sure, I turn and wave the handbag backwards and forwards, taunting him, whispering under my breath, '*Follow me. Follow me.*'

He sets off towards me, and I run. Fast enough to keep ahead, but slow enough that he won't give up the chase. At least, not yet. He mustn't give up.

I draw level with the doorway where Andy is lying, and I chuck the handbag in. It lands right by Andy's head.

The man will go to get the bag. He's bound to. Then please God he'll do the right thing.

'Call an ambulance,' I yell at the man, turning round to sprint for my life.

11

The past twelve hours have been a nightmare. I don't know what's happened to Andy, and it's tearing me in pieces. I can only think he must have died, because there was so much blood. He didn't deserve that. He didn't deserve *any* of it.

I keep thinking back to the moment I threw the bag in the doorway. Andy didn't move, but he must have felt it land. I didn't have time to check, though, because the man was nearly on me. I stopped when I got to the corner. He had given up chasing me by then, and others were gathering. His wife had called for help, and people had obviously decided that she was a more likely person in need than I had been, although I'd asked for exactly the same thing.

I had intended to wait, to see if an ambulance would come. But one of the helpers saw me, and he started to run down the alley towards me. They probably thought I did it – that I had stabbed Andy.

He saved my life, and I don't even know if he's dead. He didn't need to do that for me. He should have run.

Once I knew I was safe, I pulled the envelope out of my pocket. More than ever, I wished I had pushed Andy to tell me why he was *doing* all this for me. Nobody had ever looked after me like he had – at least, not since my mum died.

The instructions Andy had written for me were incredible. He said I should get the train from Piccadilly to Stockport. There are trains all the time, he had written, but he'd also put the time of the last train, so I walked there as quickly as I could, keeping to main roads this time. If anybody was looking for me, they wouldn't attack me on a busy street and even if they followed me I was only going to the station and not to our pitch, where I would be easy meat. I was never going back there. There wasn't anything to take anyway. I didn't exactly have a wardrobe full of clothes.

I went into the toilet at the station and managed to get most of the blood off my hands and my cheeks from when I'd kissed Andy. I stared at my lips in the mirror, and saw the bottom one start to turn down. My nose was burning and my eyes stinging. I didn't have time to cry, though. If I did, everything that Andy had done would be wasted. I whipped my top off and put it on back to front. My hoody kept the blood-spattered back covered.

I bought a ticket from the machine and took the last train.

By the time I got to Stockport it was too late to get a bus to Emma's house – so I was going to have to wait for the first one in the morning. I knew where there were some dense bushes and I could hide under those until morning – they would keep the frost off, at least.

I didn't sleep. I kept seeing Andy, lying in that doorway, not moving. I was doing what he wanted, but I ached inside at losing him.

The bus left on time, but I didn't catch it. I watched it pull out of the bus station and waited for the next. I didn't catch that one either. *What if he was wrong?*

I looked down at Andy's notes and realised that I owed it to him at least to try. I had to trust him.

There was another bus just before noon, so I forced my reluctant legs forwards, paid for my ticket and sat down at the back of the bus, my hands clasped tightly between my knees.

The bus dropped me about a mile from the house. I felt a strange fluttering inside. All this time, me and Andy had been focusing on the fact that Emma says she wants me back. But what if she's been lying? What if she wants to beat the shit out of me for stealing her baby and getting her mixed up in all that crap last year – forcing her to steal to save her baby's life? And what about him – my dad?

I'm still not sure. I keep repeating over and over, 'Andy wanted me to do this. I'm doing it for him.'

But there's another reason why I have to see Emma. I need to know whether Andy is still alive, and the only chance I have of finding that out is to ask Emma if Tom can check the hospitals.

So here I am, about twenty minutes' walk from home – if that's what you'd call it – and shaking so much it's hard to put one foot in front of the other. The shops in the small town where the bus dropped me are full of things for Christmas, and I remember coming here with my mum when I was little. She loved these shops – said they were far better than the big department stores in Manchester because everything they sold was specially chosen by the people who work here. They were chosen with love, and we had to buy them with love.

We had bought presents for everybody who went to the party on the last day – the party we were coming home from when she died. The party my dad didn't come to because he was too busy planning our kidnap.

I remember the party at Granddad's. Mummy was sad because my dad didn't come with us, but she smiled at everybody and said how hard he worked all the time. She kept looking at her watch, though, and I knew she wanted to go home. She didn't like driving at night and she wasn't looking forward to the journey. I had heard her trying to persuade my dad to come with us.

'What happens if the car breaks down in the middle of nowhere?' she had asked.

'It's not going to, Caroline. It's a new car.'

'I might have a flat tyre, and I might not get a signal on my phone.'

'Call me when you leave your father's house. If you're not home when I expect you, I'll come and find you. You'll be fine, darling. Just remember to call me when you set off.'

Of course he had needed that information. He had needed to tell the men who were going to ambush us what time we would be driving along that dark, icy stretch of road. It was all part of his plan. And it worked – but not in the way he thought.

When Mummy had seen a car blocking the road, she was going to stop. But then she got a call on her phone and she put her foot down. She had to go up on the grass verge to get round it and she was going really fast. I remember being terrified. I could see her eyes in the mirror, glancing at me to make sure I was all right – and then it happened. The car started to go all over the road, the back end where I was sitting was swinging from side to side. Then it started to turn over, and she screamed. I was strapped in my car seat, upside down. I banged my head, but that was all. I shouted for her, but she didn't answer. All I could hear was the radio, playing Christmas music.

I was crying. I wanted my mummy, and she wasn't saying anything. Her head was half out of the window and I could see her eyes were open, but she wasn't looking at me. I didn't know what that meant, back then.

Suddenly there was a lot of shouting; I could see strange-looking people coming towards the car. I know now that they looked weird because the car was upside down and they looked like they were walking on their heads, but back then it was so scary I could hardly breathe. Somebody leaned into the car and undid my car seat. I fell out and bumped my head again. I heard somebody say, 'What are we going to do with the fucking kid?' and then I was shoved at a man who grabbed me roughly under the arms.

Even after all this time I can remember his smell. It didn't mean much to me then – only that I didn't like it. But now I recognise it as Rory's smell – a horrible mixture of old sweat, too many fags and stale beer. He chucked me into the back of a car, and all the time I was crying because I wanted my mummy. I soon learned to stop doing that, though. They told me she was dead, but it was a long time before I really understood what that meant. For ages I woke up every morning thinking, 'Today's the day Mummy will come for me.'

My dad hadn't planned that my mum would die. I know that now. It was supposed to be a fake kidnap so he could pretend to the police that he was forced to rob his own company. He thought we would just be locked up for a couple of hours, and that no harm would be done while he got the money he needed.

Remembering that day and what my dad did makes me angry again. How am I going to cope with seeing him? I brush the thought aside and set off walking, knowing that I have to pass the exact spot where the accident happened – where she was killed.

Another memory leaps into my head. Just before she turned the car over, Mummy was shouting into the phone. She was shouting '*Jack*' at the top of her voice, and when I told Emma it had seemed to mean something to her – and to the policeman, Tom. But I didn't know what. All I know is that, whoever Jack is, I hate him almost as much as I hate my dad. If

Jack hadn't spoken to her, maybe she would still be alive today.

I trudge along the road, glad it's not raining. I don't want to arrive soaking wet through. It was raining last time I arrived here, but that time Rory had brought me – delivered me like some sort of parcel.

We had arrived on the back of his motorbike. He was so proud of that bike, but I hated it. I always leaned the wrong way, and he got mad. That day, though, he was less angry with me than usual because I had a job to do. I wasn't nervous. I was sure what I was doing was the right thing – all I had to do was refuse to tell my dad or the police about my life for the previous six years and where I had been living, and then as soon as I could I had to find the opportunity to take Ollie from the house. It was no big deal – I owed my dad nothing.

When Rory dropped me off down the lane from the house I had taken off the big waterproof and my helmet and handed them to him.

'Get in there, girl,' he had said. 'You can come home as soon as you've done your job.'

It's hard to believe now, but I had ached to go to the place that had been home to me for more than six years – back to Rory's house with the filthy sheets and the smell of stale food; back to clouts around the head and demands to nick more stuff from the supermarket; back to being thrown in the Pit when I did something wrong.

I suddenly remember that I never did tell Andy about the Pit. I'm glad. He didn't need to know that.

I can see the house now, up ahead. It looks just the same, the old red brick giving the house a snug, secure feel to it that almost makes me smile when I think about the bad stuff that went on in there. I didn't live there for long, but I look at the windows and know exactly which room lies behind each of them. Of course, we spent most of our time in the massive extension at the back of the house. Emma always called it the kitchen, but it had a huge dining table and a couple of comfy sofas too, with toys for Ollie and a flat-screen television on the wall. I can't see it from here; just the window of the rarely used sitting room – the room in which I faced my dad with everything I knew about him.

My dad's Range Rover isn't in the drive. Perhaps he sold it after that night. Perhaps the police took it away. There's only one car and that's Emma's. He must be at work.

I dart into the bushes, suddenly scared that I might be seen from the window – and then I realise how stupid I'm being. They are going to have to see me some time. But I'm not ready yet.

Will I ever be?

I pull my black hood up over my head, scared the sun will catch my white face. I want to be sure Emma is on her own before anybody sees me.

Instead of going up to the front door, I make my way down the muddy lane that runs along the side of the house. Not that it's muddy today. It's in the shade from the overhanging trees, so there is still frost on the ground, forming ice on top of the puddles and turning the mud hard.

I stop still and catch my breath. Emma is outside in the garden, hanging some washing out in the sunshine. I can see her through the thick hedge – just make out the red of her jumper.

I'm not making a sound, but suddenly Emma stops – her hands reaching up to the line. She freezes for a moment, and if I move slightly I can just make out her face. She seems to be listening, as if she's heard something. But it's not me. I am as silent as a mouse.

I see her shake her head, obviously deciding whatever she thought she heard, or perhaps sensed, she was wrong.

I'm safe for a few more minutes, but I need to find courage from somewhere. I need to do this – for Andy, if not for me. He believed that Emma meant every word of it; that she really does want me back. I find it harder to trust her – but I want to know. I need her to forgive me for what I did, because I'm not sure I will ever forgive myself.

12

'Come on, Ollie, eat your lunch,' Emma said as she put the spoon back in his hand for the third time. He was usually the easiest child to feed and loved whatever she put in front of him, but today he was playing up.

Emma felt unsettled today too. It was just one of those days when she felt twitchy but didn't know why. Her conversation with Tom the other night had unnerved her, and for the first time since everything happened she was beginning to think she would have to move house. Stuck out here in the middle of nowhere, she never saw anybody, and it wasn't healthy for Ollie either. She needed to be somewhere with people around her. She had only stayed here because of Tasha, in the hope that her stepdaughter would come home. This was the only place she knew to find her way back to, but even though Emma had now seen and spoken briefly to Tasha, the girl seemed further away than ever.

Emma sighed. When Tasha had called Emma had hoped that maybe she had finally started to get through to the girl, and perhaps after all this time

Tasha had realised that Emma really did love her. Maybe she should give it until March. Then it would be a year since David had died and Tasha had left. She couldn't help thinking too that it would be a year since Jack had reappeared, fleetingly, in her life. Too many things had happened in such a short space of time, but after a year with no change, perhaps that would be the right time to move on.

Her reverie was interrupted by the sound of the doorbell, and Emma jumped.

For God's sake, calm down. What was the matter with her – she was jumping at her own shadow this morning.

She pushed her chair back from the table. 'Eat your lunch, Ollie. We're going out later, don't forget. I'll be back in a minute.'

She left the kitchen door ajar so she could hear Ollie and made her way down the hall. Nobody ever came here unannounced, and she had no idea who it could be. She had meant to have a peep hole installed but had never got round to it, so she put the chain on – knowing that if somebody wanted to kick it in at that point there would be little resistance – and opened the door a crack.

A man and a woman were standing there.

'Good afternoon. It's Mrs Joseph, isn't it? Do you have a moment?'

Emma realised that she must look slightly deranged peering through the crack in the door, and these people looked harmless enough. The woman was wearing what Emma would describe as a sensible navy-blue skirt, just below the knee, and a blazer in a rather startling fuchsia colour. The man wore a sober-looking suit, and she couldn't think what on earth they could want with her. She pushed the door to and released the chain before opening it fully.

'What can I do for you?' she asked.

'No, Mrs Joseph, I think it's more a case of what we can do for you.' He reached a hand into his briefcase and pulled out a slim magazine, passing it across to Emma.

Just then Emma heard a shout from the kitchen. Ollie was obviously getting bored. She had promised him that as soon as he had finished his lunch, they would go and search for Tasha again. She had worked hard at trying to keep his sister alive for Ollie, and he seemed to respond well. He was clearly ready to go, because he was shouting her name. 'Tasha, Tasha.'

Emma looked down at the magazine the man was handing to her. *The Watch Tower.*

'I'm so sorry,' she said. 'My little boy is shouting, and I'm afraid I'm not interested.'

The man looked as if he were about to say something else – no doubt they were used to this response and he had his next line ready. But Emma didn't give him chance. With an apologetic smile, she pushed the door closed. It felt rude, but she needed to get back to Ollie.

'Okay, Ollie. I'm coming, sweetheart.'

She walked back along the corridor to where the door was ajar.

Ollie was right where she had left him, but now a hooded figure stood behind him, two black-clad arms wound around his neck.

13

Ollie. He's even cuter than I remember, and as I push the back door open and look at him, he turns towards me and beams, recognising me even with my hood obscuring most of my face. He always did seem to love me, even though I didn't deserve it, and I owe this baby so much. He nearly died because of me.

'Tasha, Tasha,' he shouts, and I run across the kitchen and wrap my filthy arms around his little body, my back to the door in the hall.

I hear a gasp behind me.

'Get off my baby. Get your filthy hands off my baby.'

I feel the rush of air as Emma lunges for me, dragging me away from Ollie.

Ollie starts to scream, and I fall to the floor, face down. I shouldn't have come. I knew Andy was wrong. She just wants me dead.

I hear her footsteps as she races to the kitchen drawer and I guess she's gone for a knife – just like the last time I found myself here, in her kitchen. I don't bother to get up. I just lie, face down, my heart ready to break in two. This was my last chance – my only chance now that Andy has gone. And we were so wrong.

'Get on your feet,' Emma says. 'Get up and go and stand by that wall at the end of the kitchen, your hands behind your back. I've got a knife, and I'll use it if you try anything.'

Ollie is still screaming, and it's hard to make out what Emma is saying – but I get the idea, and I do as she says, keeping my back to her. I don't want her to see the tears streaming down my face – to see how she is killing me. I lift my hands to try to wipe them.

'Keep your hands behind your back,' she shouts.

I reach the wall and stand facing it. I hear her drag a chair – the one with the screaming Ollie on it, no doubt – across the floor to where she thinks he's safe.

'Turn round very slowly, and no clever moves with your hands. Do you hear me?'

Oh, I hear her. I hear the fear and hatred in her voice, and I can't bear to turn round, to show her how much she's hurt me. All that pretence for all these months, saying how much she misses me and wants me back – it was just because she wants me to suffer.

I don't think I care any more. They can send me to prison or to a special remand place, or whatever they do with kids like me. I just don't care. My mum died, Izzy died and now Andy's dead. I'm best out of it.

I sniff loudly and try to raise my shoulder high enough to wipe my tears, but I can't do it. My hood falls back, and I feel exposed. I take a deep breath, and feel the shudders run through my body. Slowly, head down, I turn – too ashamed to let her see my face.

For a moment, there's silence. She's saying nothing – just standing there. I keep my eyes to the ground. I don't want to see the disgust on her face.

Then she whispers, her voice no more than a breath with a question mark. 'Tasha?'

She didn't know. She didn't know it was me. She hadn't seen my face, only my back. I lift my head slowly, tears dripping from my chin, and I look at her. She runs towards me, the knife in her hand. I stand still, not knowing or caring what's about to happen. I just stare into her eyes.

'Tasha!' she screams, dropping the knife and flinging her arms around my shoulders, pulling me to her and holding me so tightly I can hardly breathe. 'Tasha,' she repeats, more quietly now. 'Oh, thank God.'

Nobody has hugged me like this since the time I was very small and my mum thought she had lost me in Kendals in Manchester. When she found me, I started to cry and she thought it was because I was scared. I wasn't. She was hurting me.

But now I like the hurt. I've been standing with my arms behind my back, but slowly I bring them round to the front, not sure if it's okay for me to hug Emma back, but I don't think she'll mind. I put my arms round her back, loosely to start with, but as she hugs me so fiercely and cries onto the top of my shorn head, I feel the dam inside me explode as the years of pent-up terror and unhappiness gush through the gaping hole in the walls that have held me together for so long. I start to sob.

I cling on to Emma for dear life. I want to stay here, wrapped in her arms forever.

I don't know how long we stay like that, but gradually the mood changes. Emma's delight moves to one of deep concern as she realises the depths of my pain, and her hugs become gentler as she stokes my hair and whispers words of comfort against my ear.

'Shh, darling, you're safe now,' she says. And for just a moment I believe her.

I know Emma has contacted the policeman – Tom. I heard her speaking to him on the phone after we had all calmed down and my crying had stopped. I don't know how long I cried for, but Emma says it was nearly an hour. And she held me the whole time, dragging Ollie towards us so he could join in.

When she told me she had spoken to Tom, she saw the fear in my eyes and she understood.

'Tasha, you are not in trouble with the police. I promise you. They've been looking for you, but only because they were worried about you and they want your help. Tom will explain.'

I start to cry again. If she was right, two of my reasons for running away no longer counted. Emma didn't hate me, and the police weren't going to arrest me.

We haven't really talked. She's just said that now I'm back, I'm home for good – no arguing. I haven't asked what my dad will think of that, and I don't really want to see him. I'm not sure how that's going to work. I want to be with Emma, but I don't think I can stay with him. She hasn't phoned him yet – she only called Tom, so I think she must know I don't want to see him. I don't want anything to change the feeling that's in the room right now. It feels like love to me.

Emma pulls up a chair next to me and grabs my hands.

'Tasha, you need to understand that although I'm not your mum and I know I will never replace her – I wouldn't even try – I do love you and you're part of this family with me and Ollie. Okay? Don't ever, ever, run away from us again. Do you understand?'

I look at her for a moment, and slowly nod my head. But I don't understand. Not really.

It's as if a light has suddenly been switched on because her eyes open wide.

'I'm so sorry Tasha,' she says, taking her bottom lip between her teeth. One hand slides up my arms and she cups the back of my neck. In an instant I know what she's going to say, and when she speaks the words they're not a shock.

'Your dad died a couple of days after you disappeared.' Her arm moves round my shoulder and she pulls me a little closer.

I don't know what to feel. I remember loving my dad when I was little, but he did a terrible thing – he betrayed me and Mum. I didn't come back for him, but it suddenly hits me that I've got nobody now. Nobody that I really belong to.

I look at Ollie, so cute, so chubby, and now fatherless. I don't know how he died and I want to ask Emma, but I have no doubt that it was because of me and I don't want to hear her say the words.

'I'm sorry, Emma,' I say, my voice catching again.

'Sweetheart, none of this is your fault. You have to believe me. You were a victim, okay? And just because your dad's not here it makes no difference to you, me and Ollie. We're a family. I'm going to keep saying that until you believe me. I'll tell you everything, but first we need to get you used to being around here and starting to feel settled. And I want to know about you, too – where you've been, how you've been living.'

She thinks she wants to know, but I'm not going to tell her how it really was. She wouldn't like it, and it would only make her cry.

I'm saved from having to make up a rosy version of my life by the doorbell ringing.

'I hope that's Tom and not those bloody Jehovah's Witnesses again,' she says. 'Mind you, they would probably claim that God brought you back here.'

'It was the number 87 bus,' I say with an attempt at humour. Emma smiles as she makes her way to the door.

I can tell by her voice that it's Tom. She sounds excited, and I am beginning to believe that she is genuinely thrilled to have me back. She told me it was okay for her to contact Tom – that he wasn't going to arrest me. But I'm not so sure.

The door to the kitchen is pushed open, and I stare warily at this big man. At a shout of 'Ay' from Ollie – a habit he has clearly not got out of – Tom briefly turns his attention to the little guy and ruffles his hair, then turns to me with a smile.

'Hi, Tasha,' he says, his voice gentle. 'It's good to see you.'

I think that's a good sign, but something tells me this is just the sweetener, and any time soon there's going to be a blow that will hit me twice as hard, because now Emma has softened me up.

14

Tasha looked appalling. Tom had thought she had looked bad enough after a few years living with Rory and Donna Slater, but that was nothing to what he saw in front of him now. She had always been small and slight for her age, but after eight months of living rough she was practically skeletal, and he doubted if she weighed 6 stone – the equivalent of two reasonably heavy suitcases. Her cropped hair made her head look tiny, and the dark tone drained any colour she had in her face, except for her nose, which was red from crying.

But she was alive – and Emma was clearly overjoyed.

He had been half longing for the moment for Emma's sake and half dreading it – because he knew it wasn't going to be as simple as Emma thought. He had tried to tell her this a hundred times, but she wouldn't have any of it.

'There are a few things we need to talk about,' he said as they all sat down around the table. Emma didn't wait for him to start.

'I know what you're going to say, Tom, and I've been thinking about it. We'll go away for a little holiday – that will solve all the problems. By the time we're back, it will all be over.'

Tasha was looking from one to the other, a slightly wary look on her tear-streaked face at the thought that there were problems.

'Tasha,' Tom said, 'I would prefer to have this conversation with Emma while you're in the room, because I think it's really important that you don't think anybody's hiding anything from you or lying to you. You have to trust us – me, Emma, the police, social services – all of us.'

Tom caught Emma's look. 'Social services – what's it got to do with them?'

Tom sighed. He had anticipated this but not managed to deal with it well. Emma had just ignored every breath he had uttered on the subject.

'We have to tell them she's back, Emma. She's a minor and you don't have parental responsibility for her.'

'Yes I do. I'm her stepmother.'

'Well, actually no you don't – whatever you would like to believe. You can apply for it, but you don't have it by default, and Tasha has never lived with you – barring those unfortunate days earlier in the year. So we have to tell them, or you'll be breaking the law.'

Tom could see Emma's mouth set in a determined line, and he decided to deal with that later.

'Of more concern is the immediate threat to Tasha, and by association, to you and Ollie.'

Tasha's head shot up.

'But nobody knows I'm here.'

It was clear that Emma had said nothing to Tasha about Finn McGuinness or the phone call she had received, and Tom knew he had to play this carefully.

'Not at the moment, that's true. But I'm going to ask if you'll do something, Tasha, something that will help us to send Finn McGuinness to prison for a very long time. You might want to say no, but if you're considered to be competent as a witness, and I can't see any reason why you wouldn't be, you can be compelled by the prosecution to be a witness in his trial. You see you're the only person who can irrefutably tie him to Ollie's kidnap. You understand that all charges against you have already been dropped, don't you? You're not in trouble with the police. We know you acted under duress – but we really need your help.'

Tasha looked terrified.

'It will be our job to keep you safe. I know Finn is evil, and you're right to be scared of him and what he can do – even from prison – but we'll take care of you.'

Tasha looked down at her hands where she was picking at a hangnail.

'He's got people looking for me,' she said quietly.

Just as he had done eight months ago, Tom felt a swell of emotion when he looked at this kid and thought of the suffering she had endured.

'We know,' he said gently. 'They phoned Emma, to say they're watching the house – but we don't think they've got people looking 24/7 – more a random check.'

'They killed Andy.'

Tom nearly missed it, she spoke so quietly. *What the hell?* He leaned forwards and rested his arms on the table, speaking softly. 'Who's Andy, Tasha?'

Without lifting her head and speaking in little more than a whisper, Tasha told Tom what Andy had done for her: how he had tried to protect her, and how he had been stabbed in the gut for his trouble.

Was there no end to this girl's suffering?

'Would you like me to try to find out what happened to him?'

Tasha's head shot up. 'Would you do that for me?' she asked. 'Really? If you do that for me, I'll say whatever you tell me to say to the courts. Please – will you?'

Tom nodded. 'Of course. But you don't have to say what I want you to. You just have to tell the truth. That's all anybody would ever ask of you, Tasha.'

'So what happens now?' Emma asked.

'When were you next planning to go and shout Tasha's name in central Manchester?'

'This afternoon – about now, actually.'

'Do you follow a pattern?' Tom asked.

'Well, it's not a strict pattern, but I usually go the same days because those are the days when we're not doing something else. So, a sort of pattern.'

'So go,' Tom said.

Emma looked as if he had punched her.

'What, and leave Tasha on her first day home? She needs me, Tom. I can't do that. She's in pieces.'

'Yes you can. I'm not working this week – I've taken a few days' leave. I'll stay with Tasha. Stick to your routine, and they won't come looking. If you go into town today, it won't occur to them that Tasha's here. In the meantime, we'll work out somewhere to take Tasha for her own protection.'

'Wait a minute. You don't take Tasha anywhere without me and Ollie. We're a family – we all go.'

'I think it would be wise if Tasha was taken into protective custody, Emma. Just until the trial's over.'

'And then? Will it make any difference if McGuinness goes to prison? Won't he want revenge then?'

'Let's take it a step at a time.'

Tom turned to look at Tasha. The girl looked terrified, and Emma had clearly picked up on this too.

'Tom, the safe option might be protective custody. But I don't think it's the right option for Tasha. She needs the security of a home.' Emma turned to Tasha and gave her a gentle smile. 'She needs to feel loved – and she is loved.'

Tom said nothing for a minute. He couldn't force anybody into protective custody, and emotions were running high. He was going to have to come up with a plan, but for now it would have to be one step at a time.

'Go to Manchester. I'll stay with Tasha. She can have a soak in the bath, and then we'll have a talk through what might happen in court. I'll contact social services too – and don't pull that face, Emma. It absolutely has to happen. Then we'll see where we're up to by the end of the afternoon. We all want what's best for Tasha, so let's not forget that.'

Tom tried not to look at Tasha's face. She was scared, and he knew she had every right to be.

15

Tom's nice. He doesn't seem like a policeman and he doesn't look like one either. He's wearing dark-blue jeans and a black jumper that looks like it would be soft as a kitten. I've not touched it, of course, although I nearly hugged him when he said he was going to try to find out about Andy. I can hear the murmur of his voice when I'm in the bath, because the bathroom's right over the kitchen – but I can't hear what he is saying.

I don't stay long in the lovely, soapy hot water. I could have stayed for hours, but I want to know about Andy, so I dry myself quickly. Wrapped in a towel I cross the landing to go to the room I used to sleep in. I don't know if it is still my room, but I hope so.

I push the door open and stand, staring into a room I hardly recognise. I look over my shoulder to make sure I've got the right door. But I know it's for me. I don't know how she did it, but Emma has decorated the room that I have been holding in my imagination for years. Only she's done a better job.

I've never had my own bedroom – well, at least not since I was six years old. But I've dreamed about it. The one thing I've wanted more than anything was to feel it was clean – not like the foul-smelling, musty bedroom at the Slaters', where I doubt if the sheets were changed as often as once a year. Emma has somehow understood this. She's painted the walls a very pale green like new apples before they're ripe, and it feels as if the room is inviting me in and welcoming me. I take another step, hoping and praying that I'm not wrong – that this really is for me. As I walk barefoot across the pale, soft carpet, I see there is a tree stencil like the one in Ollie's bedroom, but more flowery and detailed, painted in white and covering the wall behind the bed. The bedding looks so crisp and bright it would be a shame to sleep on it. I turn round and round, trying to absorb every detail. All the furniture is an even paler shade of green than the walls – almost white but not quite – and there is a huge splash of colour from the throw and cushions piled on the bed. They seem to have been made from pieces of random fabric in bright shades of everything from turquoise to deep pink, in stripes, flowers and geometric shapes.

I sit down cautiously on the edge of the bed, scared to disturb the perfection. Has Emma done this for me? Could I have been living here all this time?

I stand up again and walk over to the wardrobe. I pause for a moment, clutching the handle, scared to look inside in case somebody else's clothes are there – some other girl that I don't know about. I hold my breath and open the door. Inside are all the clothes Emma bought for me in the few days I was here earlier in the year, some still in their packaging. I pull open drawers at random, and find the same. Underwear, socks, jumpers – all clean and ready to wear.

I don't want to leave this magical place, but I want to know about Andy, so quickly I grab some clothes. The leggings are a bit short now – I must have grown. But they're baggy, of course. I don't care – because one thing they are is clean.

When I get downstairs, Tom is making me something to eat. He says I look like I need fattening up a bit, so he's made me a huge dish of macaroni cheese with crispy bacon on top, and he gives me a big glass of cold milk. It's really delicious, but now he says we need to talk.

'The next few days and weeks aren't going to be easy, Tasha, and I'm not going to pretend otherwise. Until we get Finn McGuinness sent down we have to accept the fact that you are going to need to be kept safe. As I said, I'm afraid you're the only person that can tie him without question to Ollie's abduction. At least, the only person who might be willing to say so. Once he's been sent down, we can monitor his communications with the outside world and make sure you come to no harm.'

I don't know what to say. If I don't do this, Finn will get a much shorter prison sentence. I know it. But if I do speak against him, will I ever be safe? Will Emma? Will Ollie?

'What are you thinking, Tasha?'

I'm not sure if I should tell him what I'm frightened of, so I play for time.

'Did you find out about Andy?'

Tom nods. 'I've spoken to Becky, my inspector. Do you remember Becky? She's going to make some phone calls, and as soon as we know anything, I'll tell you. I promise. It was very smart of you to do what you did. I wouldn't normally praise somebody for stealing a handbag, but in your case it was a really bright idea.'

He looks at me and smiles, and I know he's waiting for the answer to his question about what's worrying me.

'If I say something in court about Finn, he's going to want to get me, isn't he?' I don't know why I'm asking a question that I already know the answer to.

'He'll be locked up, so Finn won't be able to get to you. But I won't deny that he has contacts outside prison – other members of the same gang or people that are just plain scared of him. He and Rory were just one part of that organised crime group. You might not know this, but they all answered to a boss – a man called Guy Bentley. He's dead – but somebody else will have taken over. We're going to look after you, though, I promise.'

I still don't really know what that means. Will they look after me until the trial or after the trial or both? Will they look after Emma and Ollie too? And for how long?

I should leave here and go somewhere different where nobody gets hurt just by being with me. I should go to London or Leeds – somewhere where nobody has ever heard of Tasha Joseph. I don't know if I'm strong enough to walk away from all of this, though, from my one chance of a family.

And maybe nowhere is safe.

16

It was freezing cold in central Manchester, and Emma was glad of it because it gave her a reasonable excuse for not staying long. Nobody would think it odd that she only shouted about Tasha for fifteen minutes instead of the usual half hour – especially with a toddler sitting shivering in his pushchair.

He wasn't cold, of course. He was snug as a bug in a rug, to be honest – but still, it made a good excuse. She couldn't wait to get back to see Tasha and wondered if she had discovered her room yet. Emma had loved doing it. To her it was a sort of talisman – its special magic working hard to bring Tasha home. She had thought about buying new clothes, but teenage girls change size and shape so quickly, and she didn't know when Tasha would be home. She had only known, without any doubt, that one day she would be back. And now she was. Emma hugged the thought to her, thinking of all she was going to do to take away the pain of her last few years.

As she drove home she was so busy thinking about what treats she could make for Tasha and Ollie's tea that she didn't notice until the last moment the strange car parked in her drive. It wasn't Tom's. His was further in, closer to the house.

For a moment, Emma felt a rush of dread. Whoever it was, it seemed Tom had let them into the house. Were he and Tasha safe?

She pulled up behind the car, blocking it in. Whoever it was, they weren't getting out of there until she – Emma – said so.

She jumped out of the car and lifted Ollie from his chair, trying to root one-handed through her bag for the front door keys.

She unlocked the door and pushed it open with her hip, anxious to know what was going on and who was in her house. As she pushed the door closed, she heard voices coming from the kitchen – the deep rumble of Tom's voice and the lighter, higher tone of a woman. She breathed again. A woman didn't seem so threatening. Maybe it was one of Tom's colleagues.

Emma lowered Ollie to the ground so that he could trot along at his own pace – which was usually at a bit of a run. Ever since he had started to walk he had had a tendency to put his head down and charge, rather than walk at a normal speed, and this time he was heading straight for the kitchen door. He had pushed it open and was through before Emma could take her coat off.

'Wow, Ollie, that was some entrance,' she heard Tom say with a laugh. Definitely not an unwelcome visitor, then.

With a smile, Emma followed Ollie through the door, and Tom and the woman both stood up. Emma glanced from one to the other, and then at Tasha. Apart from the fact that the girl looked clean, there was something else. She seemed nervous and uncertain – not the girl Emma had left, and much more like the child of eight months ago. Emma's ready smile collapsed, and she gave Tasha a questioning look. Tasha looked down at her hands.

What was going on?

The woman was holding out her hand. 'Mrs Joseph, I'm Elizabeth Webster from social services. Mr Douglas called me with the exciting news that Tasha is here, safe and sound. Congratulations. You must be thrilled.'

Emma glanced at Tom, who had the grace to look slightly sheepish, and then she turned to face Elizabeth Webster. 'I am absolutely delighted to have my family back together again, Mrs Webster. Tom told me you would have to be informed, but I didn't really expect to see you so soon.'

She glared at Tom again.

'I said before you went out that we needed to inform social services, Emma, and that I would make the call. We want Tasha to give evidence in a court case, and at the moment nobody has parental responsibility for her. That could make the whole thing impossible, so we can't afford to hang around. On top of that, we need to keep you all safe.'

'I can take responsibility for her. I told you that, Tom. She's my family – so if you need her for anything, you can ask me.'

There was silence for a moment, and then Elizabeth Webster started to speak – slowly and calmly, in a voice that Emma guessed she must have been taught to use for tricky moments.

'Mrs Joseph – Emma – we completely understand your desire to look after Natasha. It's such good news for the girl, and in time I'm sure we can make that happen. But for now …'

'What do you mean, in time? She's here *now*.'

'Come and sit down, Emma, and let me explain what's got to happen.' The social services woman smiled reassuringly.

Emma just glared at her and stayed standing.

'I am sure that if you apply for parental responsibility, eventually it will be granted. But we need to do a risk assessment first.'

'What risk? A risk to me? A risk to Tasha? I don't know what you're talking about.'

'We're not worried about a risk to you. It's the children we're concerned about, and in view of the events of earlier this year we do have to assess the situation very carefully to make sure that neither child is at risk.'

'Mrs Webster, I have spent months trying to find Tasha, to bring her home. I love Tasha. *We* love Tasha. Do you think she's at risk from *me*? I'm not going to harm her. Come every day, if you want to. Check she's not got a mark on her, and that she's happy. Ollie adores her. Look – do your risk assessment if you have to, but don't scare her. She's had a tough enough time as it is.'

Emma saw a glance pass between the social worker and Tom.

'The thing is, Emma, social services need to take Tasha to somewhere secure,' Tom said. 'They can assess her there and keep her safe at the same time. You can apply for parental responsibility and when the assessment is done, everything will be above board and she can come home. If you don't follow the rules, you're putting your chances of *ever* being granted parental responsibility in jeopardy, and then you would lose Tasha for good. And that's not what you want, is it?'

Emma felt herself boil over.

'No it bloody isn't, as you very well know. But for the record, you, Tom Douglas, or should I call you Judas, are worse than she is.' Emma pointed at the social worker.

Suddenly Tom seemed to change from the friend who was looking slightly embarrassed to the policeman he was, intent on doing the right thing. The conciliatory tone disappeared. He was now all business, his voice firm.

'Call me what you like, Emma, but I've told you many times that this would have to happen. My concern is to ensure that all three of you are safe, and frankly pretending you can ignore everything that happened earlier this year is naive. Tasha, we know, has had a terrible time, and none of this is her fault.

Everybody – not just you – wants what's best for her. If you follow the rules for a short time, you *will* get your happy family, and I will do anything and everything I can to make that happen. But don't obstruct Elizabeth. It's not helping anybody.'

Emma was quiet for a moment. Then her chin went up.

'And I if I say that you're not taking her – that Tasha's staying here with me? What then?' she said, forcing a tight smile.

Elizabeth glanced at Tom and then looked Emma straight in the eye, a flash of compassion warning Emma that she wasn't going to like what the social worker had to say.

'Emma, I'm so sorry, but we cannot – whatever you say or think – leave Tasha in the same house as Ollie until we've done our assessment. You must understand why that is. We have a duty of care to both of these children, and if you insist that Tasha stays, then I'll have no choice but to take Ollie to somewhere we know he'll be safe.'

The room is silent. Nobody seems capable of speaking, and Emma has gone the colour of my bedroom walls.

They want to take Ollie. If she keeps me, they will take Ollie! How can that be right?

I think I need to do something, but I don't know what, so I just sit and stare at everybody. I can feel my heart pounding. After everything Emma's done and all the stuff with Andy, they're going to take me away – because there's no way that Ollie is going anywhere, and we all know that.

Finally, Emma finds her voice, and it's as if she is inside my head. She says exactly what I expect her to say.

'You're not taking Ollie.' Her voice is dangerously quiet.

'Fine. I understand that, Emma, but then we do have to take Natasha. As I said, we just have to be sure she's no risk to your son.'

'Oh, come on. Of course she's not a risk to Ollie. Do you think I would have her in the house if I believed that she would ever do anything to hurt him? Do you seriously think I would risk Ollie's life or well-being in any way if I thought there was a problem? Of course I wouldn't.'

The Elizabeth woman just stands, her sympathetic smile fixed in place, and waits. But Emma hasn't finished.

'Tasha has had a terrible life, and none of it has been her fault. She lived through more than six years of hell after she was abducted and has just lived another eight months on the streets. This isn't the time to make her feel unloved and unwanted. She'll just run away again, and all of this – everything I've tried to do – will have been for nothing.' Emma's voice breaks on the last bit of the sentence, and I feel myself tense. I know what's coming.

'She won't run away from us, Emma.' There is total confidence in the woman's voice.

Emma's brows go down in the middle. She's puzzled, but I'm not. It means I'll be placed somewhere secure, where I can't do any harm to anybody – in particular to Ollie.

Tom at least seems to realise that I'm still in the room, and he turns to me, sitting down again so he's at the same height as me and he can look me in the eye.

'Tasha, neither Emma nor I believe you're a threat to Ollie – but that doesn't mean we can ignore the system. If you want to be part of this family there are things that have to be done properly, otherwise you could be taken away again in the future. That's all we're trying to do here. Make sure everything is sorted so that you can stay here forever. I promise, there's no sinister plan. And we do need to keep you safe – not from anybody in this house, but you're well aware of the threats from outside this room, aren't you?'

I know he's right, but I want to stay here so much in my lovely room with my cute little brother. I want Emma to care for me and hug me again, every day. When she held me so tightly, it felt as if all my pain and unhappiness were escaping, seeping out through my skin.

It doesn't matter what I want, though.

I put both hands on the table and push myself back.

'What are you doing?' Emma asks, her voice sharp.

'Getting my coat.' What did she expect me to do?

'Sit down, Tasha. You're not going anywhere. I've told you.'

I see the Elizabeth woman bite the corner of her lip. She's not pleased with Emma – that's obvious.

'Emma, we can go round and round in circles as often as you like, but if Natasha stays here, Ollie has to come with me. I'm sorry – I really don't have a choice.'

I start to get up again, but Emma flaps her hand at me.

'You are asking me to choose between my children.'

The woman gives her a funny look, which I think means what are you talking about – you've only got one child. Emma obviously gets the same message, and I can see the anger in her eyes.

'As far as I'm concerned, these are both my children, and choosing one over the other isn't acceptable.'

'Come on now, Emma. You're making this far more difficult than it needs to be. Ollie is your son.'

'Of course he is. And from this point forwards, Tasha is my daughter. If I choose Ollie, what message is that giving Tasha? That she's not as important as her brother?'

'I understand how difficult it is for you. I'd like to think Tasha will understand why we have to do this and will appreciate that it's only for a short time. That might be harder for a two-year-old to grasp, don't you think?'

Emma was fighting so hard for me, and although I knew what the outcome was going to be, it was kind of her at least to try.

She starts to pace the room, not speaking, head down, hands on hips. She's thinking, but I have no idea what her plan might be.

Suddenly she stops and spins round, facing the Elizabeth woman.

'What about if Tasha stayed with me, and Ollie went to stay with somebody that I choose – somebody responsible who you could totally trust?'

The woman puts her head on one side. Her bottom lip sticks out as if she's thinking, and her face looks like one of those pug dogs. I can hear Andy whispering in my ear, 'Not a good look on her, is it.' I push thoughts of Andy to the back of my mind for now, because the woman has sorted out her face and is talking, but she starting to sound impatient, as if she's keen to get on – to take me away.

'I don't think that would work. There aren't many people that we could have total confidence in. Let's just get this over with, shall we?'

Emma bends down and picks Ollie up. She holds him tightly to her and whispers against his sparse hair, kissing his little pink cheeks. All I can hear is 'I love you, little man – and I'll see you very soon.'

With that, she walks over to Tom.

'Your godson, I believe.' Emma turns to pug-face. 'Is a detective chief inspector, who happens to be on leave this week and who is also Ollie's godfather, good enough for you, Elizabeth?'

I can't believe she's doing this. And she's doing it for me.

17

After Tom had gone home with Ollie and pug-face had sucked in her lips and left, clearly not at all happy with the outcome, Emma and I had spent the evening in silence. She tried to make conversation, but I was too upset. Not for me – I was hurting for her. What had she done?

I told her over and over that I would go, but she wouldn't let me talk about it. She found something on the television that neither of us wanted to watch, but it filled the silence – the emptiness of the house without Ollie. We sat cuddled together on the sofa and pretended we were interested in a diving expedition in Antarctica.

In the end, we went to bed early: Emma because I am sure she thought the sooner she was asleep, the sooner it would be tomorrow, when Tom could bring Ollie for a visit; me because I couldn't stand the pain I seem to cause to everybody I touch. But I couldn't sleep. My head was spinning, my thoughts hopping from one thing to another – never settling before racing off to somewhere else. I couldn't quite grasp them as they flew by.

Emma loves me. Emma kept me instead of Ollie. I've got a home. I should leave for their sakes. What's happening to Andy? It's my fault Emma has lost Ollie again. I never want to leave here. Finn McGuinness – he'll stare at me in court with those glassy, black eyes, and I'll freeze.

I had never been so comfortable in a bed before. Even when I was here last time I didn't have a new, soft mattress like this one – just the old one that had been there for years. When Emma redecorated this room, she bought a brand new bed – just for me. I'm so used to hard, cold floors that to start with it felt as if the mattress was going to swallow me whole. But I fidgeted around for a bit and settled in, burrowing down beneath the big, soft duvet.

It made no difference, though. My head was spinning, and each time I drifted off, I jerked awake again.

At some point during the night I must have finally dropped off to sleep, and I woke needing the bathroom. I had drunk more water, milk and juice in the past few hours than I had in weeks, and I crept silently from my bedroom – scared of waking Emma.

I needn't have worried.

Her door was ajar, as was Ollie's, and I remembered that she always left them like this so she could hear her little boy if he cried in the night.

But she wouldn't be hearing him tonight.

From Emma's room there was a sound, muffled by pillows, but it was a sound I knew well.

Emma was crying, weeping for her lovely baby, who should have been there with her. He should be here, not me, I thought. I bet she can't help being reminded of that time just a few months ago when she thought she had lost Ollie for good – because of me.

I stood on the landing for minutes, listening to her sobs. More than anything I wanted to go into her room and climb into bed, put my arms round her and offer her some comfort. But she might push me away.

I waited, trying to decide what to do, but I couldn't go in. It wasn't me she wanted.

I thought again about leaving – running away, back to a life underground. I thought about the cold, the hunger, the odd bite of food on a good day. But if I went, Emma's life could get back to normal. It would be the right thing to do.

My body felt heavy, as if a weight was pressing down on me, on my chest, on my head, and I went back into my bedroom and silently began to get dressed. I got as far as the landing before I remembered.

Before we came to bed, Emma said she had set the alarm, and I didn't know the code. She had locked the door with a key, which she had removed and taken with her. We both knew why – but neither of us said a word.

I stood, looking down over the bannister, knowing that I could find a way out if I really wanted to. But I didn't. I could pretend I was locked in, but really I knew it was an excuse to stay.

I went back to my room and lay down, fully dressed, curled up into the tightest ball I could manage, waiting for morning.

Emma was up really early. I heard her, but I thought seeing me would remind her that I'm the reason Ollie's not here, so I lay on the bed until she knocked on my door. I pretended I had just that minute finished getting dressed.

We haven't talked about her unhappiness this morning, but she's obviously tried to cover her red eyes with more makeup than she usually wears.

Tom is bringing Ollie round for a visit – which social services have allowed as long as Tom stays here too. I don't blame them for this. They don't know me, and they don't know that I would die rather than hurt Ollie. Emma looks at her watch every two minutes.

Tom is doing some shopping as well. He says that until something has been worked out – and I know he means protection – none of us should leave the house, and I have to keep away from windows. We don't want anybody to know that I'm here and from tonight we are going to have policemen staying downstairs in the house to keep us safe – all in preparation for the court case.

18

The November weather was pressing down on Emma. It was raining again today – a cold, thin drizzle oozing out of grey skies and driving the hardiest of people indoors. Miserable was the best word to describe it, and it matched her mood.

She wanted to be elated because of Tasha – and in many ways she was. This was what she had fought for, and now she had the girl back with her. But she should have listened to Tom. He had told her it wasn't going to be plain sailing, but she had believed that her love and her desperate need to make up to the girl for such a terrible childhood would be enough to persuade social services to do the right thing.

It seems they didn't doubt her intent – but they were concerned for Ollie, and he had to be protected. She couldn't have let them take Tasha, though – like a stone cracking a windscreen, the girl's last shred of hope and trust would have shattered into a million pieces.

Elizabeth had promised the assessment wouldn't take long, but Emma was terrified of the outcome.

Much as she was missing Ollie, she knew he would be safe with Tom. What had kept her awake was the thought that at some point she might have to break every promise she had ever made to Tasha. Each time she closed her eyes the scene in which she was forced to say goodbye to her stepdaughter played out in her mind, and the tears wouldn't stop, so Emma had decided to get up at 6 a.m. and do some cleaning. Nowhere needed it, but she had to do something.

More than anything, she wished she had somebody to talk to. There was always Tom, but, good friend that he was, she didn't feel able to open her whole heart to him – to bare her soul. And she was still a bit mad at him, even though she knew everything he had said and done was right.

He had looked aghast when she had presented him with Ollie but he had risen to the challenge. She knew he liked babies and had always hoped he would have more. His daughter Lucy was growing up fast, and Tom was a man who should have a family around him. A pity things with that Leo girl seemed to have gone off the boil, although Tom still refused to talk about it.

That was typical of Emma and Tom's relationship, really. They were friends, but they held so much of themselves back. The only person Emma had ever been truly herself with was Jack. She recognised now that her relationship with Tasha's and Ollie's father had been emotionally undemanding, which had been precisely what she had wanted and needed at that time. They had got along just fine, and David had been a thoughtful and considerate husband, although she had acknowledged to herself that at some point during their brief marriage she had realised he was a weak man. She just hadn't known quite how weak.

It had been different with Jack. He saw into her soul, and the only way he had been able to stop her from seeing into his was by running away. He should have trusted her to help him deal with the mistakes he had made.

Emma threw the cleaning sponge into the sink and dried her hands. She couldn't talk to Jack – she had no idea where he was or how to contact him – but she couldn't help hoping that if she poured her heart out in a note on her computer, he would read it. She didn't know how often he sneakily logged into her computer, but she was certain that he was reading the sticky notes on her desktop. That would be his style – his way of checking on her to make sure she was okay.

She sat down at the table and opened her laptop. As it sprang to life, she wondered what she could say – what words she could use that, to anybody else, would look like her own private musings, but to Jack would mean so much more.

She opened a new sticky, and began to compose her note as if she were writing a journal.

Yesterday I got Tasha back. And I lost Ollie. I never thought I would lose him again, but social services said they had to protect the children, and until they are confident that Tasha isn't a risk, one or the other of them had to go. So now Tom has got Ollie, and I miss him so much that I keep having to wrap my arms around my body to hold myself together. I feel as if I have a wide open space inside me, hollow and empty. But Tasha can't know this. She needs reassurance that she is just as important to me.

Tom wants her to give evidence against Finn McGuinness, and I know that people are looking for her. His people. They contacted me. They threatened me, and Ollie. I don't know where it's going to end, because convicting him isn't going to make him lie down. He'll want revenge, and I don't know what to do. Tom says he'll keep us safe, but will McGuinness ever give up?

She stopped writing. Emma had no idea whether Jack would see this. Had she been dreaming when she thought he had moved things around on her desktop? Maybe the computer did that automatically. It had given her such comfort to think that she could share her thoughts with him, but now she realised that it was probably just wishful thinking.

19

The prison guard stood with his back to the wall, trying – as he had been taught – to be unobtrusive. He was only here to deal with any problems that might break out. And it sometimes happened. Wives came to see their husbands, and occasionally their disappointment overflowed to the point of a punch to the head. He never blamed the women for this. Imagine finding out you're married to a scumbag? Mind you, most of the wives already knew. But there were always a few who were shocked to find out that things weren't quite the way they had always hoped they would be with their very own Mr Wonderful.

Today, though, the guard kept his eyes fixed firmly on Finn McGuinness and his visitor – a young chap who had been before to see this prisoner, and the guard didn't like the look of their body language.

When he had taken this job, he had decided to try to learn about body language so he could spot things brewing. He had tried to learn lip-reading too, but McGuinness had grown a beard and a moustache. He barely opened his thin lips when he spoke, and his words even at close quarters were muffled by the hairs that practically covered his mouth.

Right now he was leaning forwards, saying something to his visitor, who shot back in his chair as if he had been head-butted.

'Are you sure?' The guard could make out the words of the clean-shaven man.

McGuinness's eyes turned blacker than ever with a spark of anger that nobody would like to have directed their way. The young man looked a bit sick as he listened and then nodded once.

He slid out from behind the table, unable to push his seat back because it was bolted to the floor, and said something that looked to the guard like 'consider it done.'

McGuinness was up to something, and the guard wished to God he knew what it was.

20

Emma is pacing the floor, looking at her watch every few minutes. The pug-faced Elizabeth woman came to see me again for an hour this morning, asking me questions. I presume she's 'assessing' me. For some reason I felt the urge to blank her. I wanted to go back to being that kid who came here all those months ago – the kid who ignored everybody and refused to speak. Sometimes it feels safer not to care what anybody else thinks of you, and when she asked me a question I let my face settle into an uninterested sneer.

Then I saw the look of horror on Emma's face. *What are you doing?* the face said, and I almost gasped out loud at my own stupidity.

This is where I want to be. I have to be brave and let them get to the heart of me, perhaps a place where nobody has been for a long time. Except Izzy. And maybe Andy.

I've started to get jittery since she left. Tom will be here soon, and he should have some news about Andy. If he's dead that will be something else that's my fault. He shouldn't have protected me. He should have let them get me. It would have saved Emma a lot of pain, that's for sure.

The doorbell rings and Emma runs, almost skidding on the wooden hall floor, to answer the door.

'Ollie,' she cries, and I hear a chuckle from Ollie and a shout of 'Mummy' followed by a disgruntled 'Ay'. I guess she squeezed him too tightly.

Emma is practically dancing as she makes her way into the kitchen, with a smiling Tom in her wake. Her world is complete again, and I slouch down in my chair, trying not to be noticed.

'Ollie – say hi to Tasha,' Emma says, not allowing me to stay outside of her circle. Ollie unwraps his arms from Emma's neck and turns, reaching out to me instead.

Emma smiles. 'Take him, Tasha. Give him a cuddle – he gives great cuddles, don't you Ollie?'

I slowly push my chair back and walk round the table.

'Tasha,' Ollie shouts, reaching out further.

I look from Emma to Tom, trying to decide if it really is all right, or whether pug-face will reappear miraculously and whip the baby out of my arms. They both nod their encouragement, and I pull his warm little body close.

He nearly strangles me with the strength of his grip around my neck and plants a very wet kiss on my cheek, which makes me laugh out loud. I see Emma's eyes fill with tears, as if there haven't been enough of those, and I squash my nose into Ollie's pudgy cheek and give him a kiss back. I hand him back to Emma, not because I ever want to let go of him, but because I can see her hands are twitching by her sides as she tries to prevent herself from grabbing him back to squeeze him some more.

Tom comes towards me and reaches out a hand to touch me gently on the arm.

'I've got some news for you, Tasha. It's about Andy.'

I feel a shiver run up my spine. *Please don't be dead, Andy.*

'We've found him, and he's okay. Well, that's a bit of an exaggeration. When he was admitted to hospital he was critical – he'd lost a lot of blood – but your intervention with the handbag was better than you could have ever dreamed. The guy who chased you found Andy, and his wife – the woman whose handbag you stole – turned out to be a doctor. Between them they managed to stem the flow of blood until the ambulance arrived. She went with him to the hospital and basically saved his life.'

I don't know what to say and I feel myself begin to shake. Tom reaches out to me and lowers me gently onto a chair.

'I'm sorry it's taken us a while to get the good news to you, but I wanted to be absolutely certain we had the right boy. Believe it or not there was more than one stabbing in Manchester that night.'

Andy. My head is full of pictures of him – laughing when he brought back a warm meat and potato pie one day that he'd kept hot inside his hoodie.

His top never stopped smelling of gravy after that, because of course we could never wash any clothes. We just wore the same ones until we managed to find or nick something new. Then there was the time that he stood up to that man and nearly got his throat slit. And the mental image of him begging on the street and exposing his twisted arm to get me some money nearly makes me cry.

'Becky Robinson went to see him in hospital,' Tom says. 'She told him you're safe and well, and he was very happy to hear that. I guess that boy really looked out for you, didn't he?'

I don't know what to say. He saved my life.

'He told Becky why he'd run away and he said he'd always felt bad about keeping it from you. The thing is, he's a proud lad and he didn't want you to feel sorry for him. But now he thinks he'd feel better if you know. Do you want me to tell you?'

I can't speak. I do want to know, but it's going to hurt because I've always known he has suffered and I can't stand to think of Andy's pain. Tom waits, and finally I nod my head.

I let Tom's words flow around me, hearing them but not really absorbing them. He tells me how Andy's father was a respectable businessman, so when Andy was injured over the years nobody suspected his father was hurting him – he just joked about how clumsy his son was.

Tom carries on, and still I try not to focus on Andy's pain.

Later. I'll think about it later.

'His mother wasn't able to protect him,' Tom says, 'She was scared herself, and I think she tried to blot it all out – to pretend it wasn't happening.'

He pauses, and I know the worst is yet to come. His voice becomes gentle, and quieter, and yet each word punches a hole in the barrier to my friend's pain that I am hiding behind.

'Then Andy's sister died. She was very unhappy, and Andy thinks he should have known what she was planning to do so he could have helped her, protected her.'

Oh, Andy.

'Was the father hitting her too?' I ask.

'No. He was hurting her, but in a different way.'

Tom doesn't need to say more. Abuse of that kind was all too common in the world I grew up in.

'Andy had no idea, and when his sister decided to take her own life he attacked his father. His arm got broken in the fight, but he just stuck it in a sling and left home the same day.'

I can't get the mental image out of my mind. It's as if it's on a loop – Andy making himself a sling, trying to pack a bag with one arm, walking out of the kind of house I imagine he lived in, and off down the road without looking back. Over and over it plays, while Tom's words wash over me as he tells me the rest: the father's prison sentence; the mother's rehab; the new home and family that they're going to find for Andy.

I realise that I will probably never see Andy again but I'm happy for him. He's going to be safe too, and I know I'm never going to forget him.

I suddenly feel so lucky. However crap my life has been, at least I had my mum for six years, then Izzy and now Emma and Ollie. And at the worst time in my life I had Andy – a boy who had never had a happy day in his life, but whose only wish was to protect me because he hadn't been able to save his sister.

For the first time ever, I feel as if nothing else can go wrong for me now.

Neither Tasha nor Emma looked as if they had slept a wink, as far as Tom could see. He was sorry for them and the added stress they were going through, but if they wanted to be a family then a few more hoops had to be negotiated.

Tasha's face as he told her the news about her friend, though, was a picture. When this was all over, perhaps he would be able to find a way for the two kids to be in touch with each other.

Andy's wish to protect Tasha meant he had told her one lie that Tom wasn't going to divulge. She believed him to be fourteen, but he was actually only twelve.

Tom was sure Andy had said he was older so Tasha would let him look after her. If she'd known he was younger, she would have thought she had to look after him, and that wasn't what he wanted. Tom hoped that by saving Tasha the way he did, Andy might now be able to forgive himself for failing to save his sister – something that was in no way his fault.

He was a brave lad, and braver than Tasha realised. Becky Robinson had been shocked by what she saw when she visited Andy in hospital.

'Tom – he was lying in bed with bandages around his stomach, so his chest and arms were bare. He's got loads of tiny scars all over his upper body – deep pink, shiny areas. The nurse said they're all cigarette burns. She let slip, although she probably shouldn't have, that as well as the broken arm at some stage his ribs have been broken too, possibly more than once.'

Tom would personally have liked to seek out the father of this boy – a kid so brave he had risked his own life for his friend – and knock the bastard from here to next week. Of course, he couldn't do that. But he had checked and discovered the father had been given a fifteen-year prison sentence. Not long enough, in Tom's opinion, but it was something.

Now, though, Tom had to push all of that to the back of his mind and focus on the issue of keeping Emma and Tasha safe from whatever he was certain Finn McGuinness was going to throw at them. The only saving grace was that Tom couldn't think of any way that McGuinness could know that Tasha was home.

21

Finn McGuinness's visitor made his way onto the busy concourse of Piccadilly Station, and straight to the public phone box. The smell of fresh bagels from the nearby shop wafted his way, drowning out the usual smells of too many bodies in one place, and his stomach rumbled. He couldn't face food right now, though. He was about to do something that might sign his own death warrant.

He fed money into the machine and dialled a number he had memorised, piling additional coins up ready, should they be needed.

The ringing tone at the other end of the phone sounded strange, but he didn't have time to think about that because it stopped after two rings and he felt beads of sweat erupt from his top lip and forehead. He wiped the hand that wasn't holding the phone on the leg of his jeans.

'Well?' a voice said.

'I've seen him.'

'I know you have.' He should have guessed that he couldn't lie, or pretend things were different to how they were. 'And?'

'He's had the word – someone from social services on his payroll, I guess.'

'And the plan is?'

The visitor hurriedly explained what he was expected to do and when, hating himself for the tremor in his voice.

'If I don't do it,' he said, 'that bastard McGuinness will have me tracked down. I'm *dead* if I don't do it.'

'Then do it,' was the unexpected response.

He couldn't have heard that right. He had thought this was going to be his way out – his way of escaping McGuinness's grasp – and all he would have to do was report the plan to the man on the phone, take the money on offer and then do a runner. He wanted out.

He had thought himself so cool when he was recruited by the gang when he was just fifteen. The simple tasks he had been given to begin with had escalated to occasional acts of brutality, but nothing on this scale. And now he was being told to go through with it by the person he had thought would save him.

'Are you sure?' he asked. He had thought this bloke was one of the good guys, but maybe he'd got it wrong.

'Yes – do it. But not until I say so. I need some time – call me again in two hours.'

The phone went dead.

The man replaced the receiver and walked out into the concourse, the smell of the bagels now making him feel physically sick. He should have tried harder to find the girl in the first place and done what he'd been told to do. She was one homeless kid. But this was a whole different ball game, and one he really didn't want to play.

22

The day Tom had spent with Emma, Ollie and Tasha had been good, and he had felt bad picking Ollie up in his arms and putting him in the child seat in the back of the car at the end of the afternoon. Emma was trying hard to put a brave face on it, and Tasha just looked guilty. The road ahead for this family was going to be fraught with difficulty, but Emma was a determined woman, and he hoped and prayed that they would make it.

Despite Emma's refusal to consider protective custody, Tom hadn't been happy to leave her house until reinforcements had arrived. Something was brewing – something he couldn't see, hear or touch, but it was happening nevertheless. He wanted two policemen on duty at the house at all times and had waited until they had been fully briefed.

At the moment the only people who knew Tasha was back were social services and the handful of police who would be used to keep an eye on Emma's house. Becky knew, of course, but he had asked her to keep a small team out on the streets looking for Tasha. Together with Emma's visit to Manchester the day before, it should be enough to convince any-body watching that Tasha was still missing.

Tom had spent some time that day coaching Tasha. Not to put words into her mouth, but to give her an idea of how the questioning might go – par-ticularly from McGuinness's defence counsel. They wouldn't go easy on her because she was a kid. She was nervous and anxious, but her answers had been clear, and Tom was confident that she would do a good job at the trial.

Emma hated the fact that they were virtually under house arrest, but without Ollie at her side she couldn't keep up her previous performance in the city centre.

'Can't I even go to the shops?' Emma had asked, her frustration clear.

'You can't take Tasha, and you can't leave her here on her own. So I'll do it for you,' Tom had offered as he left the house. 'I'll go now, and bring you the stuff tomorrow.'

'Okay, Ollie?' Tom said over his shoulder to the little boy strapped into his chair in the back of the car as he drove along, heading for the supermarket.

'Kay,' came the high-pitched voice. Tom smiled. Ollie was a placid kid and no trouble really.

He pulled the car into the car park, picked up Ollie and sat him in the back of a trolley, his chubby little legs swinging.

'Come on, then,' he said to the little boy. 'Let's go and get some bits and pieces for your mum and something for our tea, shall we?'

Ollie nodded, and rocked his head from side to side as Tom pushed him – clearly enjoying the view from this height. He beamed at everybody who passed, and most of them grinned back.

Tom was selecting some nappies for Ollie when it happened.

He had his back to the aisle, and the voice came from behind his back.

'Tom Douglas?'

Tom turned round. A man in bike leathers and a helmet – visor down – was standing behind him, holding out an envelope.

'This is for you.'

Tom frowned and kept his hands by his side. 'Who are you? And how did you know where to find me?'

There was no answer.

Tom wasn't going to take the envelope until he knew more.

'Which company do you work for?' he asked.

The man – fairly young by the look of his slim body – waved the envelope again. When Tom still didn't take it, he spoke.

'I was told you might be difficult. So just read the front of the envelope, and then take it.'

The man turned the envelope over, and Tom felt the blood drain from his face. His hand shot out to take the envelope. This couldn't be happening. It couldn't be real. He glanced up at the young man, but all he saw was his back, disappearing into the crowd of shoppers, and his eyes were drawn back to the envelope he was holding.

Five words, that was all. But enough to send a flash of ice down Tom's back.

23

The man parked his motorbike – the one he had nicked from Rory Slater on the basis that he wouldn't be needing it for a while – in the woods just down the road from Emma Joseph's house. This was his second trip of the day, and the final one. From here, there really was no going back.

After his visit to the prison that morning and the subsequent phone calls, he had been on a mission, collecting supplies from all the names he had been given. He didn't feel as if he'd had a moment to give any serious thought to what he was about to do, and he knew if he stopped to think, he might falter.

There had been too much to carry on the bike in a single trip, so he had travelled here earlier that evening after darkness had fallen, creeping silently into the woods, hiding the first batch of purchases under a shrub, covering them with the still fresh autumn leaves. It was unlikely anybody would be walking here on such a cold, miserable night – but he couldn't be sure, so his supplies had to be concealed well.

It was now half past two, and the time seemed about right. Even people who have trouble sleeping have usually nodded off by now, and it was too soon for the early awakeners. He reckoned he had about an hour to do everything necessary.

He picked up both backpack sprayers and put one over each shoulder. He could carry the bag of bottles wrapped in bubble wrap in his left hand and before he picked up his small equipment bag in the other, he pulled down his balaclava. With the exception of a white patch around his eyes, his leathers and head covering allowed him to blend into the night. Even his two white plastic backpacks had been wrapped in black polythene.

He set off through the dark woodland, leaning forwards slightly to accommodate his burdens but also to help him peer into the shadowy depths between the trees and find his way. He couldn't use a torch – nobody must see him.

The most dangerous stretch for him was the small section of road that he would have to walk along to reach the house, but few vehicles came this way, and he would see their headlights approaching, lighting up the night sky, before they saw him.

As he drew close to the house, he could see two cars parked in the drive. One, he knew, was Emma Joseph's. The other was a police car. He had been warned that the police would be here, protecting the girl.

He made his way towards the front of the house, keeping to the grass to avoid any sound of footfalls on the gravel path. There was a light on in a room at the front of the house, and he guessed that would be where the police had positioned themselves. His first job was to cut off the door from that room into the hall.

Leaving the two backpacks and the bag of bubble wrap on the lawn, he made his way around the back of the house, carefully, silently, reaching over to unbolt the side gate. There were no lights in the kitchen or upstairs, and the house seemed peaceful, its usual occupants no doubt deep in a dreamless sleep. He hoped so – and that they stayed that way. Only the policemen in the sitting room would be awake.

He was relieved to discover that the back door had a number of small panes of double-glazed glass, which would be ideal for his purposes – much better than having to remove a whole window. He took out some tools, gently prised off the beading from around one of the panes and carefully removed the glass, placing it on the floor. He then returned to the front of the house, where he had already discovered that next to the front door were panes of decorative glass. Once again he removed the beading from around one of these, working silently until an empty hole gave him the access he needed. He could just hear a murmur in the background and realised that the policemen were watching the television. He needed to move quickly in case one of them left the sitting room.

He picked up one of the backpacks – the one marked with a small white X in the top corner – and started to walk around the outside of the house, spraying the wooden window frames, down the brickwork and along the base of the wall. An area of wooden facing boards at the back of the extension received special attention because he knew that the brickwork would allow some of the liquid to be absorbed and therefore might not be as effective as he would like.

Round at the back of the house, he took the second backpack and extended the arm to the maximum, pushing it through the empty window frame and through the cat flap to a different part of the kitchen to spray the wooden furniture as best he could. He sprayed up into the air for good measure, knowing that the droplets would ignite and create a ball of fire high up, which would begin to work its way through to the bedrooms. The gaping holes in the windows would help too – oxygen had to be in constant supply to keep the fire burning.

Praying that the smell wouldn't penetrate until he had finished his preparations for the front of the house, he quickly returned to the porch entrance and began to spray the inside of the hallway, giving the area around the sitting-room door extra attention.

He had decided that paraffin was a better option for the inside of the house because it didn't evaporate as quickly as petrol, a potential problem inside a warm house. The wooden floors in the hall were ideal, because carpet might have soaked too much of the liquid, and every drop was going to count here. He had used petrol for the outside.

The extension arm for the sprayer just reached the bottom of the stairs, and he gave them an extra soaking too, to make it difficult for people to go up or down.

He needed to make sure that the sitting-room door was blocked before he did anything else. He checked his pocket to make sure his handgun was there – just in case the police made it out through the door – but that was a last resort. He extracted two bottles from the bag and removed the bubble wrap. Strapped to each bottle was a package containing sugar and potassium chlorate. Inside was a mixture of petrol and sulphuric acid. He knew that when the bottle broke, the acid would react with the contents of the package and produce a white hot flame, which would in turn ignite the petrol. This would light the paraffin-soaked floors, and finally he would then set fire to the trail of petrol around the house.

Nobody would be getting out of here alive.

Leaning through the window, he aimed the first of the Molotov cocktails at the legs of a console table, and the specially made thin glass of the bottle shattered on impact. A ball of flame erupted in seconds, and he leaned in to throw another one against the door. It didn't break.

'Shit,' he muttered. But the heat of the burning paraffin would get to it soon, and it wouldn't be long before it exploded.

He quickly lit a match and, standing well back, threw it into a pool of petrol by the front door.

Racing round the back, he grabbed the last two bottles and hurled them through the empty window frame in two different directions. He heard one break against the worktop, but didn't hang about to find out about the other. He threw another match at the petrol at the back of the house, although the flames from the front were already taking hold, and he picked up the two spray backpacks and flung them towards the house in the sure knowledge that they would burn off any evidence that he may have left on them. There was no point in removing them from the scene. There would be no doubt that this was arson.

For a moment, he was worried. The flames were licking around the outside, but apart from the flash of the flames as each Molotov had exploded, there didn't seem to be much happening.

He waited. Surely somebody would have heard the bottles breaking by now and would be investigating? He looked up to the first floor, expecting to see lights coming on. But the electrics wouldn't work any longer – some of the power points would have burned through, and the fuses would have tripped out. As he ran back around the house, sure enough the lights in the front room had gone out. The occupants of the house were probably frantic with fear, desperate to rescue the baby. He thought he heard a scream, but it might have been his imagination, or a distant owl.

A sense of nausea washed over him, and he knew it was time to get out of there.

As he backed away, mesmerised by the fire, there was a whoosh, and a wall of flame lit up the inside of the hall. The second Molotov, no doubt. He thought he saw a woman's face at the end of the hall, and as the lad reversed down the path, his eyes never leaving the sight before him, he watched to see if whoever it was would escape. But nobody came.

He could see the window frames he had sprayed with petrol burning fiercely, showing the outline of each pane as if the house had been lit up for Christmas. The first window blew in, providing more oxygen to the air-starved rooms, and within seconds the whole of the downstairs of the house was alight – the flames burning brightly.

Time to go, he thought. As he turned and ran towards his waiting motorbike, he stumbled, his legs weakened by the knowledge that he had just murdered five people.

24

The call from Detective Superintendent Philippa Stanley's office came more quickly than Tom had expected the next morning. She was demanding his presence, and there was no way he could avoid facing the music. The fact that he was on leave for the week made no difference, and he hadn't really expected it to.

He knocked once on her door and pushed it open. His boss looked at him, and he noticed her startled expression at his appearance. He knew his face was white, his eyes like dark holes – he had barely recognised himself before he left the house. Apart from a brief frown, though, she didn't acknowledge Tom's obvious distress.

'Tom – we've got things to talk about. Sit down.'

He didn't. He pulled two envelopes from his pocket and handed them to Philippa. She opened the top one first and looked up at Tom, her mouth settling into a hard line.

'What's this?'

'You can see what it is, Philippa. It's my resignation.' Tom's voice was quiet. It wasn't a moment that he was enjoying.

Without another word, she looked at the second envelope, pulled the single sheet of paper out and scanned it. This time, she struggled to contain her surprise. Then her face settled.

'And the resignation is because of this?' she asked. Tom just looked back at her.

Neither of them had time to say another word as, following a perfunctory knock, Philippa Stanley's door burst open, and Becky Robinson practically ran into the office.

Becky was white.

'Sorry, ma'am. I didn't know DCI Douglas was with you.'

'It's okay, DI Robinson. You look upset. What can I do for you?'

Becky looked uncharacteristically flustered. 'Err, no – err, can I speak to you in private, please?' She gave Tom a look that he couldn't interpret.

'Is that entirely necessary, Becky?' Philippa said, relaxing her formal attitude slightly. Becky's gaze just kept flicking back to Tom.

'For God's sake, Becky – what is it?' Tom asked.

She took a deep breath. 'I'm really sorry, Tom – but that fire last night. It was Emma Joseph's house.'

'I know it was,' he said, keeping his voice level.

'Well, I don't know how to say this, but according to the news it's been leaked that they've found bodies. Oh shit, Tom, I'm so sorry – but they're all dead.' Becky burst into tears.

25

It had taken quite some time for Becky to gain control of her noisy sobbing, and in the meantime, Philippa had switched on the news. It appeared the fire brigade was denying adamantly that they had put out any statement about bodies, claiming that they were still sifting through the debris.

'Unfortunately the fire has done considerable damage, and the roof has fallen in. We know that a family lived there, and we know that at this point in time their whereabouts is unknown. But I can confirm that as yet we have found no bodies. I don't know where this rumour has come from.'

'We understand that some communication between members of your team was intercepted,' the reporter said, 'and mention was made of these bodies. One of your men said, and I quote, "It's one of the worst parts of the job, finding the body of a dead child. You never get over it." You may not be ready to confirm this yet, Mr Concannon, but are you prepared to deny that there are bodies?'

'All I can say is that our investigation has not yet finished, but at this point there are no confirmed bodies.'

'"Confirmed" being the operative word,' the reporter said, turning to face the camera.

Philippa watched the screen for a moment longer, then used the remote to turn it off.

'I wouldn't normally say this in a matter so incredibly sensitive, Tom – but on this occasion I think Becky needs an explanation. Do you agree?'

Tom paused for a moment. Becky only knew the basic facts about Tasha's return. He hadn't told her that he was supposed to be looking after Ollie, or that Tasha was being assessed. It wasn't a police matter, and apart from asking for her help with Andy, Tom had barely spoken to Becky all week.

He had to decide how much it was safe for her to know, and certainly the fewer people that knew the truth, the better. But Tom would trust Becky with his life, so he nodded.

'It's your story, Tom – you'd better be the one to tell it.'

Becky was looking anxiously from one to the other, and Philippa handed the second of the two envelopes to Becky. She read the words on the front out loud.

White Hat
Please open immediately

Becky looked at Tom with a puzzled frown. She wasn't to know this, but only Jack had ever called

Tom White Hat. When he had been given the envelope in the supermarket he had known instantly who it was from.

'Just read it, Becky,' Tom said.

Becky pulled a single sheet of paper from the envelope, and Tom watched her eyes skim over the words. He didn't need her to read it out loud. He had memorised every sentence.

Tom

No time for sentimental chat, Little Brother – but I miss you.

Right now I need you to do something.

Please call Emma and tell her to be ready 30 minutes from now with anything that she really values from her house. But 30 minutes is all she has. The maximum.

McGuinness wants Tasha dead – no question about it – and he doesn't care who is taken down with her. We can try to foil him one attempt at a time, but we won't win.

He has paid a man to set fire to the Joseph home tonight, and I think it's in everybody's interests if that is exactly what happens.

Fortunately, I was good to this guy when he wasn't much more than a kid, before Finn got his claws into him, and he's remembered. When I knew he'd been visiting Finn in Strangeways, I knew he was up for something serious, so I contacted him. Too bad he'd already hurt that friend of Tasha's, but now the guy is mine.

He needs to do the job, and he needs to get away. I've seen to that.

In one hour – no more – bring Emma, Tasha and Ollie to Manchester airport, terminal one. Get the police out of the house too – tell them there's been a change of plan, but don't let them realise what's happening. Somehow – I'll leave it to your imagination – you need a squad car parked outside, as if they're still in there. That's what my lad will be expecting, and we don't want him to stop to ask questions.

Inside the envelope are new passports and new names for Emma, Ollie and Tasha. The tickets are waiting at the BA information desk and will only be handed to Emma in her new name.

Don't try to find out where they're going, Tom – because you'll only get half the story. From their first stop, they will be directed elsewhere, with yet another identity. Neither you nor, more importantly, Finn McGuinness, will be able to find them.

I will look after them – I think you can trust me with that.

Don't stop the fire. Finn needs to think they're dead.

Once more, Tom, I'm asking you to be the hero, and I know how sad losing them will make you.

Jack

Becky had finished reading, and she looked from Tom to Philippa, her confusion apparent.

'But Jack's dead, isn't he?' The obvious question, and Tom couldn't blame her for asking it.

'I believed so too,' Tom said. 'But it seems my brother faked his own death to escape the clutches of Finn McGuinness and his boss, Guy Bentley. Eight months ago, when he heard that Tasha was alive and being used as a lure, he came back to help us to capture Guy and of course in the process he helped us to recover Ollie. Then he disappeared again – and until now, I haven't heard from him since.'

Becky glanced at Philippa. 'You knew about this, ma'am?'

'I didn't know at the time, Becky – but when Ollie was abducted the head of Titan found out, and Tom didn't think it was appropriate for the senior officer in the Organised Crime Unit to know while I remained in the dark.'

Becky gave him a black look, and he knew she was thinking: 'But okay not to tell me?'

After a few seconds of silence, Philippa spoke again.

'How the hell did he get this message to you, Tom – given that he only gave you an hour to execute the whole thing?'

'A young guy who appeared to be – but wasn't – a motorbike courier delivered it to me in the middle of the supermarket. Jack had clearly pinged my phone to find out where I was and sent the lad there.'

'Your brother should be working for us.'

'I think he is, in his own way. I just wish it could be official so I could get him back.'

'Well, after this little performance, I would say that's looking a bit unlikely – wouldn't you?'

Tom said nothing and gave a brief nod.

'So having read Jack's instructions, what did you do?'

'I did everything he asked.'

When the biker in his leathers had handed the envelope to Tom and he had seen who it was from, he had abandoned his trolley and quickly carried an excited Ollie back to the car.

After securing Ollie, Tom had sat in the car and read the message from Jack.

Not for one moment did Tom hesitate. Jack had been clever, as always. He hadn't given Tom time to think – to work out a different strategy. If Tom hadn't taken the chance right then, it could ultimately have cost Tasha her life, if not the lives of Emma and Ollie too. He could prevent that night's fire, but for how many years could he protect them?

Philippa Stanley gave Becky what could only be called a calculating look.

'I'm sure you understand the absolute secrecy that has to surround this, DI Robinson.'

'Yes, ma'am.'

'Well, if you are feeling all right now, do you think you could leave us? DCI Douglas and I have other issues to discuss.'

Becky stood up. 'I'll catch you later,' Tom said.

He couldn't interpret the look she gave him – it seemed like a mixture of sympathy for the whole situation and disappointment that he had never told her Jack was alive.

The minute the door closed behind Becky, Philippa turned to Tom.

'Who else knows about this?' she asked.

'Nobody – just the biker guy, but I believe Jack when he says he's taken care of him.'

What Tom didn't tell her was that he had hidden in the back garden and watched the house as the flames licked upwards, crackling fiercely, the odd small blast from inside suggesting that bottles – maybe of spirits – were heating up and exploding.

Tom had stood there, the heat from the fire burning the skin of his face, wondering if he had done the right thing. He could have stopped this happening and he still couldn't be sure he had made the right choice. He had taken a risk going there, but for his own sanity he had needed to check for himself that the policemen really had done as instructed – left the house and not returned. He had enough on his conscience without the death of two of his colleagues.

Finally, with a last glance up to the bedroom where Ollie should have been sleeping, he had turned back towards the thick hedge that bordered the property, pushing his way through a hole he had made earlier that night before the man had arrived with his cans of flammables.

Walking quickly to the front of the house he had jumped into the police vehicle that he had borrowed earlier that evening and reversed out onto the road, pulling away from the house.

He had returned home, but not to bed. He knew he had a letter to write, and possibly the most difficult one of his life. It had taken him until sunrise to write, and now Philippa held it in her hand between finger and thumb as if it were a vital piece of evidence that she shouldn't really be touching.

'And this?'

'I've no choice, Philippa. Tasha was our means of getting McGuinness sent down for life, and I let her go. I was put in care of Ollie by social services, and I let him go too. As far as they're concerned, he should have been with me last night. It will appear that I blatantly disregarded the trust they'd put in me. I didn't consult anybody about any of this – I just did what my brother told me to.' Tom looked straight at Philippa. There was no point trying to make excuses.

'Well, I think your brother's influence is rather more extensive than you might have realised.' Philippa was almost smiling. 'The reason I called you in this morning wasn't because of the fire. I was going to tell you that there's been a change in the charges against Finn McGuinness. Clearly Tasha is out of the picture now – but Finn's wife, Julie McGuinness, is in.'

Tom's head snapped back. Julie McGuinness had been found guilty of a whole range of crimes. She had run under-aged prostitutes from one of her houses and she had been involved in the kidnapping of Ollie Joseph. Her trial hadn't been delayed, as her husband's had, because she wasn't ill. She had been given a hefty prison sentence, but had always sworn that she wouldn't give evidence against Finn.

As his wife, she couldn't be compelled to do so, and since being found guilty she had always said there was no chance of her saying a word against Finn.

'What changed her mind?' Tom asked.

'Somebody has been getting to her, explaining that with the evidence we have against him, her husband would undoubtedly go down, but for less time than she would, as he couldn't conclusively be tied to the kidnapping without a witness. I think the idea that he might get a lesser sentence than her made her blood boil, and so she's going to sell him down the river. She knows there might be repercussions, but I think in the prison she's in the other inmates will be more scared of her than she is of them, so it will be hard for Finn to find anybody to harm her. She's quite a piece of work, but somebody clearly knew how she thinks.'

'And you believe that was Jack?'

'Well, not in person, no. But she's been influenced, and my guess is that Jack's found a way of making it happen. So – you don't need to resign on that account.'

Tom smiled. 'No – there's just the fact that I allowed three people to leave the country on false passports and handed back a child that was supposed to be in my care.'

Philippa said nothing for a while and then picked up the telephone. 'Can I speak to Siobhan Lewis, please? Tell her it's Philippa Stanley.'

Tom knew exactly who Philippa was calling, but couldn't work out from what height she was about to drop him in it.

'Siobhan – thanks for taking my call,' Philippa said. 'Listen, I'm really sorry, but we had to take a very serious decision last night without consulting your team. I believe you have a colleague called Elizabeth Webster, who was dealing with the return of Natasha Joseph. Look – for reasons I can't go into right now, we've had to take the whole family into protective custody. This has to remain strictly between you and me, as you know. Ms Webster cannot be informed – nor can anybody else. I will, of course, go through the formal channels and sort the paperwork, but at this end there are only three people who know, and I would prefer it if at your end it could just be you.'

Philippa listened for a moment. 'Yes, I'm really sorry and I know it's not the right way to go about things – but you may have heard about the serious house fire in South Manchester last night? That was the Joseph home, which I suspect you will hear about any time soon from a member of your team. It was arson – the plan being to kill Tasha Joseph. So you might understand the urgency on our part.'

Tom could hear some speaking from the other end of the line but was so surprised at Philippa's actions that he didn't even try to decipher the words.

She hung up and immediately dialled another number.

'Claudette, can you call the fire service, please. I need an urgent meeting in the next hour with the chief fire officer. I'm on my way as we speak.'

Philippa pushed her chair back and stood up.

'A few loose ends to sort, and then I'll see you back here in two hours. If you believe there are any family members who genuinely need to know that Emma and Ollie are alive, and I hope there are very few of them, you need to tell them now before Mr Concannon changes his statement and it's announced to the whole world that they are well and truly dead.'

Switching on a piece of equipment standing next to her desk, Philippa picked up the first letter Tom had handed her and pushed it into the machine. The shreds fell into the bin below. She held out her hand to him, and Tom knew what she wanted. The message from Jack. Loath as he was to hand over what might be his last communication ever from his brother, he knew he had no choice.

EPILOGUE

I look around me at this strange place that Emma says is our new home. It's hot here, even though it's November, and people are speaking a language I don't recognise.

The last day has been mad. Emma got a call from Tom yesterday evening – at least, I think it was yesterday. She started rushing around, throwing things into bags. I asked what she was doing, but she put her finger to her lips. The policemen downstairs weren't to know what was going on, for some reason. But I didn't know what was going on either.

'Tasha, darling – do you trust me?' Emma asked. Well, of course I do – she let me stay instead of Ollie. How could I not trust her?

'Is there anything here that's valuable to you that you would hate to lose?' she asks me. I think of my beautiful bedroom, but I know that's a stupid thought. Then I remember the painting at the end of the hall – the one of my mother that has hung there since the day she married my dad. Emma didn't take it down even after my dad died.

I tell Emma what I'm thinking.

'Oh sweetheart,' she says. 'I'm so sorry – we can't take it. It's too big.' She gave me a hug. 'Wait a minute – I've got an idea.'

I heard her race downstairs, and after a minute or two she came running back up. 'What do you think?' she said, holding her mobile phone under my nose. She had managed to frame the picture perfectly, and the lighting was good. 'When we get where we're going, how about we get this blown up? I know it's not the same, but it's something isn't it?'

I knew we were about to leave, to go somewhere else, but I was too frightened to ask where. As long as I could be with Emma, though, I was sure it would be fine.

Ten minutes later, there was a shout from downstairs.

'Mrs Joseph?'

Emma went to the bannister that overlooked the hall.

'We're leaving now,' the policeman said. 'Mr Douglas has just pulled into the drive with Ollie. He says he's going to stay for a couple of hours, and then two new policemen will be assigned to you for tonight. Are you okay with that?'

'It's fine,' Emma shouted. 'Thanks, and we'll see you tomorrow.'

A few minutes later, Emma said to me, 'Are you ready?' I didn't want to ask 'For what?' so I just said yes.

Tom was waiting outside in the car with Ollie, and we piled in. He gave some stuff to Emma, and she turned round and spoke to me carefully.

'Tasha, I know I'm not your mum and I promise I will never try to pretend that she didn't exist. But for now – even if just for today – could you please call me Mum? We need people to believe we're a family, and I can't take you out of the country if you're not mine.'

They're getting me away, I thought. They're helping me to escape. But a sudden thought hit me. Are they taking me somewhere safe and then leaving me?

'Don't look so worried, Tasha – we're all going. Your name is Ava, mine is Clare and this little chap is Billy. But you need to call me Mum – just for now. Is that okay?'

I nodded. I didn't mind calling her Mum every day, if I was honest. The other lady – the one in the picture in the hall – had been my Mummy. A special lady, but Emma – no, sorry, Clare – was special too. And the name Billy suited Ollie.

Tom had taken us to the airport and helped settle Ollie/Billy in his pushchair. I heard him talking gently to Emma. She was crying, saying she was sorry, and Ollie's little mouth was turning down too. So I reached out my arms for him, and we walked to one side for a little, me singing a silly song about an old man and a farm that my mum used to sing to me.

Emma seemed to have calmed down a bit, so I walked back. I heard Tom explaining that she couldn't be in contact with anybody ever, but that he would get in touch with her father.

'I promise I'll explain it to him,' Tom said. 'But I wouldn't be surprised if Jack hasn't already thought of that.'

Jack?

I stopped dead in my tracks. I remember that name. What could he possibly have to do with all of this?

We had to catch two planes, and Emma picked up another envelope at the first airport. Our names had changed again, but only our surname, thank goodness. I think the first airport was somewhere in America, because people were rushing everywhere, talking like people in films, and it was so busy. I think it was called O'Hare airport – but I don't know where it was. We didn't have long to wait for our second plane, though, and now here we are – in this strange country where I don't understand a word anybody is saying. Emma says they're talking Spanish, but she says there are lots of different languages spoken in this country, so we're going to have some studying to do.

A car has been sent to pick us up. I thought Emma looked a bit disappointed by something. I'm not sure what. Perhaps she was expecting somebody to meet us. She seems both nervous and excited. She keeps banging her nails together really quickly. I can't work it out – but I don't want to ask. I'm just keeping quiet, playing with Ollie/Billy and watching.

Emma has explained to me that we're going to start a new life, and I realise that because of me, Emma has had to give up everything.

'No, Tasha, you're wrong,' she says – forgetting to call me Ava. 'Everything important to me is right here, right now. Don't ever forget that.'

The car is turning up a lane, and I sense we are nearly there – wherever 'there' is. The trees are lush and juicy looking, with fat shiny leaves – not like the trees that we left behind in Manchester, and Emma says there are monkeys here too. That makes Ollie laugh.

Emma's leaning forwards in her seat, almost willing us to get to our destination.

And there it is – ahead of us. The road stops here, so it has to be where we are going. There's a house built of wood with a bright-green roof. The mountain rises up behind, covered in the same fat-leaved trees, and down below I can see the sea. There's a veranda that goes all the way round the house, and I can see a hammock swinging from a beam. I wonder whose house this is.

A man walks out onto the veranda. He's wearing shorts, and his legs are very brown. He has a mop of wild, black, curly hair that stops just short of his shoulders, and he is smiling as if his face is going to break in two.

I hear a gasp from Emma. 'Jack,' she whispers, her voice almost cracking.

He walks towards the car and pulls the door open, reaching in a hand to help Emma out. They stand looking at each other and don't speak. He lifts his other hand and strokes her face with the back of his fingers.

'Your hair,' she says – and I can't think why on earth those are her first words to this man.

He laughs and lifts his hand to ruffle it. 'Couldn't stand the skinhead look,' he said. 'I've been growing it back.'

I'm sure they've forgotten us as they stand and stare at each other, but then they seem to remember they are not alone, and at the same time they laugh and turn back to the car. The man lifts Ollie out and passes him to Emma. Then he reaches out his hand to me. I ignore it and refuse to move until he withdraws. I can see Emma frowning, but I don't care.

Finally, I shuffle across the car seat and get out on my own. The man doesn't hold out his hand to me again, he just gives me a smile and says, 'Hi, Ava. I'm Jack.'

'I know who you are,' I say. 'You're the man who killed my mother.'

It's morning now, and I haven't slept a wink. It's a small house, and Ollie and me went to bed early – Ollie because he was tired, and me because I didn't want to be in the same room as *him*.

Jack took my outburst well and barely blinked. Emma, though, looked frightened. I don't know why.

'Ava,' she said, 'please don't think that about Jack – even for a second.'

I hate the name Ava now, because he must have chosen it.

'Don't call me Ava,' I say. Emma knows nothing. She wasn't in the car when my mother called out this man's name.

Ollie and me slept in the same bedroom, and after a while I realised that Emma wasn't going to come and take the other bed. There are only two bedrooms, so she must have been sleeping with him. I don't know how she could.

Before we went to bed, Emma had tried to explain everything to me and had started to talk about what happened with my parents – what my dad did, what happened to my mum. But Jack interrupted her.

'Leave her, Emma.' Even he can't get used to calling her Clare. 'It's been a difficult few days for her. Let's talk in the morning.'

But I don't want to talk.

I could hear Emma crying again last night. I didn't catch every word, but I did hear her say, 'I haven't got any choice, have I?' I don't know what she meant.

When I finally come out of my room and go into the living room, Emma and Jack have their arms around each other, and even Ollie is included. I stand like the spare part I am, but as soon as Emma sees me she lets go of Jack and comes over to hug me. She at least had the sense not to draw me into a hug with him.

She pulls me close and whispers in my ear. 'It's okay, Tasha. We don't have to stay. We'll find somewhere else.'

I look over her shoulder and see that our bags, what little we had with us, are packed and sitting by the door. For a moment, I feel a sense of victory but I look at Emma's face and even bring myself to look at Jack and I wonder what on earth I'm doing.

'Do you want to go?' I ask.

'I want whatever you want, Tasha. You deserve to be happy.'

So does Emma. I look at Jack, knowing that my eyes are narrowed and my mouth tight, but I'm not able to change my face. 'Sort your face out,' Rory Slater used to say when I looked miserable, angry or stroppy, and then he would clip me round the ear. This time, nobody spoke and nobody hit me.

Jack is looking back at me. He looks sad.

Slowly, I free myself from Emma's arms.

Still looking at Jack, I say two words. 'Tell me.'

And he does. He tells me all the stupid things he did when he wasn't much older than me, and how he got into a mess that he couldn't get out of. He tells me how he discovered what the plan was for me and Mummy, and how he tried to stop it.

'Jack was trying to save you both,' Emma said. 'And when the gang boss found out …'

She couldn't finish her sentence, but I knew what she meant.

'That's why I had to leave England,' Jack said, his voice soft. But I couldn't miss the sadness on his face when he looked at Emma.

I'm quiet for a moment and I remember Mummy's voice in the car that night. 'Why can't I stop?' she was shouting.

It comes to me, slowly at first and then in a rush. She was going to stop and get out of the car. That must be what they had planned – Finn, Rory and, of course, my dad. Jack had told her not to stop. He was trying to help her. He wanted her to escape, to get away from whatever was about to happen.

She was asking him for help, she was calling to Jack to save her. And because he tried to save us, he had to pretend he had been killed. He had to lose everything and everybody he cared about.

I can't speak for a moment when he's finished the story. Everybody's looking at me, not knowing what I'm going to say. Emma is leaning forwards, towards me, not touching me, but her face looks desperate. I know I have to speak – I have to make this right for everybody, not just for me. But I can only think of one thing to say.

'What's for breakfast, Mum?'

I look at the relief on Emma's face and, for the first time in a very long while, I think I've done the right thing.

About the Author

Rachel Abbott was born and raised in Manchester. She trained as a systems analyst before launching her own interactive media company in the early 1980s. After selling her company in 2000, she moved to the Le Marche region of Italy.

When six-foot snowdrifts prevented her from leaving the house for a couple of weeks, she started writing and found she couldn't stop. Since then her debut thriller, *Only the Innocent*, has become an international bestseller, reaching the number one position in the Amazon charts both in the UK and US. This was followed by the number one bestselling novels *The Back Road*, *Sleep Tight* and *Stranger Child*.

In 2015 Rachel Abbott was named the number one bestselling independent author in the UK since Amazon opened the Kindle Store five years ago, and she was also placed fourteenth in the chart which included all authors during the same period. *Stranger Child* was the most borrowed novel for the Kindle in the first half of 2015.

Rachel Abbott now lives in Alderney and writes full-time. *Nowhere Child* is a short novel that continues the story of the lead character in *Stranger Child*.

Connect with Rachel Abbott online:

If you would like to be notified of any new books by Rachel Abbott in the future, please visit http://www.rachel-abbott.com/contact/ and leave your email address.

Twitter: https://twitter.com/RachelAbbott
Facebook: http://www.facebook.com/Rachel Abbott1Writer
Website: http://www.rachel-abbott.com
Blog: http://rachelabbottwriter.wordpress.com

Acknowledgements

Whenever I put pen to paper (or more accurately, fingers to keyboard) to start a new story, one of the highlights in the first few weeks is the research. The Internet is, of course, of huge value. But there are always those difficult questions that Google doesn't seem quite able to answer, and for that I am delighted to have the help and support of a number of enthusiastic experts.

Top of that list has to be Mark Gray, who has once again steered me through some very tricky sections relating to the police and the law in general, only holding back on the advice when I strayed into confidential areas. As always, there are times in this short novel when I had to dispense with reality in the interests of the story, and so any and all inaccuracies are entirely mine. But thank you once again, Mark – without you I would have believed everything I see in TV thrillers.

As a short novel, *Nowhere Child* has had fewer early readers than usual, but a huge thanks to those who have read it – especially Judith, who read it in one afternoon and came back to me immediately with some insightful and helpful comments.

I would struggle to keep my head above water without my two excellent virtual assistants, Ceri and Alexandra. Who would have thought that VAs in Hertfordshire and Canada could work so well? But both, with their own unique style, have solved so many of the day-to-day problems of being an independently published author, and I don't know what I would do without them. I am now blessed to have a part-time PA too. Tish helps to organise my office and my life, saves me hours of administration work each week and makes me laugh out loud when I'm supposed to be planning a murder.

I must also give a special thanks to Diana and Stephen Mellor, who have allowed me to take over another room in their wonderful fort – my home in Alderney – agreeing that it could be renovated and made into the best office that anybody could wish for.

Alan Carpenter, my jacket designer, has produced yet another wonderful cover (he knows how much I appreciate him, because I never stop telling him), once again using a photo of the beautiful Alicia – who deserves special thanks for making these jackets stand out, as does Rick Hall for such great photography.

I am often asked why, as a self-published author, I need an agent. An agent like Lizzy Kremer, supported by the outstanding team at David Higham Associates, is invaluable. Her editorial input is second to none, and she remains an inspiration. Thanks to Clare, Laura, Harriet and Niko for their feedback and all-round support.

I'm also pleased to have a first-class copy editor – David Watson – who not only turned the edit round in record time, but also made some excellent observations that have undoubtedly helped me to polish the story.

It really has been a terrific team effort, and I continue to count myself lucky to be surrounded by the best group of professionals, friends and family there is.

STRANGER CHILD

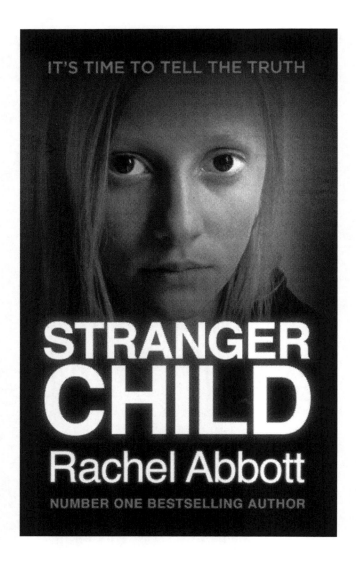

IT'S TIME TO TELL THE TRUTH

STRANGER CHILD

Rachel Abbott

NUMBER ONE BESTSELLING AUTHOR

One Dark Secret. One act of revenge.

When Emma Joseph met her husband David, he was a man shattered by grief. His first wife had been killed outright when her car veered off the road. Just as tragically, their six-year-old daughter mysteriously vanished from the scene of the accident.

Now, six years later, Emma believes the painful years are behind them. She and David have built a new life together and have a beautiful baby son, Ollie.

Then a stranger walks into their lives, and their world tilts on its axis.

Emma's life no longer feels secure. Does she know what really happened all those years ago? And why does she feel so frightened for herself and for her baby?

When a desperate Emma reaches out to her old friend DCI Tom Douglas for help, she puts all their lives in jeopardy. Before long, a web of deceit is revealed that shocks both Emma and Tom to the core.

They say you should never trust a stranger. Maybe they're right.